William C. Lawton

Art and Humanity in Homer

William C. Lawton

Art and Humanity in Homer

ISBN/EAN: 9783337369156

Printed in Europe, USA, Canada, Australia, Japan

Cover: Foto ©Andreas Hilbeck / pixelio.de

More available books at **www.hansebooks.com**

ART AND HUMANITY
IN HOMER

BY

WILLIAM CRANSTON LAWTON

New York

MACMILLAN AND CO.

AND LONDON

1896

Norwood Press
J. S. Cushing & Co. — Berwick & Smith
Norwood Mass. U.S.A.

In all Loyalty and Affection

To C. H. L.

Adelphi, February, 1896.

PREFACE

THIS group of essays approached its present form as a course of "Extension" lectures. The little book is intended in part as an illustration of the new educational movement. The syllabus originally prepared for the lectures is reprinted in an appendix, by the kind permission of the American Society for the Extension of University Teaching. It is hoped that most readers will be stimulated toward the wider course of Homeric study there indicated. If any youthful student has never yet made the acquaintance of the Iliad and Odyssey at all, he may find it necessary to do so before he can understand all the following pages.

Still, an earnest effort has been made to render these chapters intelligible, and even in a way complete, in themselves. For instance, the essay on the Underworld attempts to quote and discuss every important Homeric passage alluding to the condition of the dead. The young student is earnestly advised to read the great poems for himself with notebook in hand, seeking every allusion to one or more important and oft-recurring subjects, such as architecture and the other arts, use of metals, condition of slaves, etc. The gathering of such statistics may add to a careful reading of Homer as many-sided stimulus and instruction as would the quest for peculiar constructions or dialectic forms.

The writer firmly believes, too, that the Homeric poems (and many other masterpieces of foreign literature) should be read through, and read repeatedly, even by competent linguistic students, *in English translations.* Sustained courses of instruction in ancient literature, archæology, and art, conducted wholly in English, should be prepared for all students whose chief work is in other fields. The realization of a historic continuity in man's intellectual life is as indispensable to all educated people as

is the adequate mastery of their mother
speech or of arithmetical and algebraic
methods in computation. Toward such
serious studies, in English, the author hopes
to have contributed something, if only in
his appendix.

The present volume appeals, however,
especially, to the general public ; or, rather,
to those earnest men and women who wish
a perfectly simple and readable introduction
to the chief masterpieces of ancient literature. Perhaps it should contain more frequent references to works of archaic art.
These are, however, rarely direct illustrations to Homer. Archæology, too, is so
popular just now that one small volume of
mere literary and æsthetic criticism may
perhaps claim toleration. Moreover, the
closing essay of the present series is, in
tone at least, if not in substance, a palinode
to Archaiologia ! This paper, as is elsewhere
explained, has detached itself from the opening essay. Most of the papers appeared in
an earlier form as magazine articles in the
Atlantic Monthly.

A second volume is now nearly completed,

upon the lost Cyclic Epics, the Hesiodic
poems, the "Homeric Hymns," and in general that persistent survival of epic dialect
and metre whose manifold forms may be
best grouped as "The School of Homer."
In such a field, where no great English
versions in accessible form exist, the translator's functions — as distinguished from
exposition and criticism — will become rel-
atively more imperative and constant.

One somewhat technical question may
perhaps best be raised here. With one exception these studies are also experiments
in English hexameters. Possibly the volume would never have appeared but for its
author's interest in the old and unsolved
problem of the ideal form for a translation
of Homer.

Neither the arguments nor the masterly
English translations of the two older friends
to whom he is most indebted for encour-
agement and sympathy, Mr. Charles Eliot
Norton and Mr. George Herbert Palmer,
have convinced him that prose is the proper
form into which to translate a poem, particularly a sustained effort like an epic.

One point seems not sufficiently emphasized
in any discussion ; namely, the importance
of the *line* as a natural unit of measure for
the thought.   Any verse becomes unbear-
ably artificial and wearisome, to poet and
hearer, which is not of an approximately
fit length for the ordinary, the average
sentence or clause of the language in question.

Aristotle remarks that the iambic trimeter,
the twelve-syllable verse of Greek tragedy,
is the metrical form nearest to the language
of prose, and intimates that this is the cause
of its great success and vogue in Greek
drama.   The English speech, having lost
its inflectional endings, usually needs only
ten syllables, at most.   Hence the persistent
life of our "blank verse," and of rhymed
combinations of the same unit.

The "heroic couplet," however, passed
out of use to a great extent in England with
the coming of a less artificial poetic school,
because its instantly recurring rhyme com-
pels the expenditure of *twenty* syllables
upon the expression of a single thought.
This requires either padding of a feeble

kind,—chiefly adjectives,—or else the composition of a second line carrying an idea purely tributary to that uttered in the preceding verse.

Dante's Commedia is composed in lines of about eleven syllables. The loss of music and grace in a transfer to English is a most discouraging one. We never yet knew any one who learned to love or admire the poem first through Longfellow's version. But the ideas — Mr. Norton says we can bring over little more in any case — are there intact. More than this, Longfellow offers us the poet's thoughts in orderly succession. We confess that with all the superior faithfulness and taste of Mr. Norton's own version, despite his Dantesque accuracy in choosing the one fit word, we are often bewildered, often wearied, by the weighty thoughts falling thick and fast without the recurrent pause between. We miss the division into lines, because it was a fit and natural division. If any lover of Dante will undertake to recall his favourite passages, he will almost invariably find himself quoting *entire lines :* —

Quegli è Omero, poeta sovrano,

Lasciate ogni speranza, voi ch' entrate,

Quel giorno più non vi leggemmo avante,

and endeavouring to render them in English iambic verse.

And now, to apply all this to the case in hand. It has been already conceded that the Homeric hexameter is too long for an ordinary English sentence. That is alone enough to condemn it for use in a sustained original poem. Its accentuation is also very remote from the natural cadence of the average English sentence. Evangeline is perhaps not loved chiefly for its metre. Clough's Bothie is rugged reading. Kingsley's Andromeda is better metrically, but is a mere classical experiment in artificial form. These are not inspiring examples, and will hardly be largely followed.

In the problem of translating Homer, however, the question is both simpler and more difficult. The thoughts are furnished us, the amount a line shall express is fixed. The fatal defect of all versions in blank verse is that this unit of measure, the line, cannot be retained, and so the articulation of the thoughts is broken up. Ten English syllables cannot be made to hold the thought of the average Homeric verse. All translators make from a fifth to a half more lines. (The writer tried at first laboriously to make such line-for-line versions for the essay on the Closing Scenes of the Iliad, and held out for just twenty-one successive verses. In many passages it would be absurd to attempt it. With some hesitation the translator decided to leave this earlier attempt for the express purpose of comparison with the other rhythms essayed elsewhere.)

Now, granting all the metrical and musical diversity between the two languages, it will doubtless still be conceded, that an English dactylic line, when successful, is, at least, a closer echo of the Homeric verse than anything else in our rhythmical armoury. It was indeed a somewhat long line even for early Greek needs. Hence the frequent repetitions, the fixed epithets, etc., which are saved from the stigma of " padding " only by their unfailing grace and fitness. But here — if anywhere — the final solution

of the translator's Homeric question is to be
found.   The resonant Latin element of our
vocabulary must be largely drawn upon.
The earlier freedom in forming fresh com-
pounds might be cautiously revived.   The
naïve repetitions and epithets of Homer
should be fearlessly retained.   Perhaps successive generations of humanistic scholars
will have to use and improve upon the
results of their predecessors, as Mr. Palmer
both practises and advises.   Perchance a
great master of poetic forms will suddenly
arise to show us how simple a thing it is to
translate Homer, by simply doing it.   The
writer has little question that a translation
in hexameters, at least equal to the German
work of Voss, is attainable in English.
Perhaps, indeed, the spirited versions of
Mr. Way have already demonstrated this.

WILLIAM CRANSTON LAWTON.

ADELPHI ACADEMY, BROOKLYN,
      February 1, 1896.

CONTENTS

xvii

ART AND HUMANITY IN HOMER

HOMER

I

THE ILIAD AS A WORK OF ART

WE must still regard the Greeks as our
teachers and unrivalled masters. Not,
however, upon the whole, in the domain of
spiritual or moral truth. Here modern men
grasp firmly essential verities toward which
even Plato only darkly groped. Whatever
the destiny which may await the miraculous
side of Christian belief, yet the consciousness of brotherhood among all mankind,
based on a steadfast trust in one allwise
and beneficent Higher Power, is the priceless and inalienable gift of that faith to
humanity.

Nor shall we ever turn to the ancient

world for our models in social and political
organization. The Athenian republic of
Pericles, with its few thousand leisure-
loving citizens, standing upon the necks of
slaves tenfold their own number, and exact-
ing reluctant tribute from a confederacy of
nominally independent cities and islands,
can throw little direct light upon the infinitely larger problems which we and our
children must face. The most interesting
development of the present decade is the
vigorous assault by the educated and benevo-
lent upon the centres of poverty and crime
in our great cities. But in Plato's ideal
republic, as in the actual states he had
known, to "elevate the masses" would have
been to upheave all the foundations of
society : it would have meant preaching dis-
content and sedition to the indispensable
slaves who supported the "leisure class."

The mastery of the Greeks lay especially
in those creative arts which ennoble and
adorn the life of man, and in the harmonious development of all the physical and
mental faculties. We may hardly venture
to set definitely before ourselves a loftier

goal of progress, than the future attainment, by the citizens of the American republic, by its teeming millions of men and women, to the same capacity for refined and enlightened enjoyment of all their mental and physical powers that was reached in ancient Attica : reached, to be sure, by a mere handful, consisting of men only, and in a privileged social station.

For such reasons, as well as for many others, a poem — though it be of unknown age and authorship, though it have ever so little historical background — which was for many centuries the Bible of the Hellenic race, which nearly all Greeks gladly accepted as containing the truth in regard to their own ancestors, which furnished their loftiest ideals of heroic character and of literary art, must be eminently worthy of our attention and thoughtful study.

But the Homeric poems cannot be safely used as a handbook of early Greek history, nor even as a picture of actual Hellenic manners and customs in the age before the Olympiads. The element in these creations concerning which we can speak most definitely and positively is the Incredible. For instance, there never existed a race of heroes living on terms of familiar intercourse with the Olympian gods, exchanging wayside greetings in enchanted islands with Hermes (Odyssey, X. 277-307), or buffets with Ares on the battle-field (Iliad, V. 846-864). The hundred clans of early Hellas never set forth, willingly and harmoniously, upon a fleet as large as Xerxes', and beleaguered a foreign city for *ten years*, merely to restore one unfaithful woman to her rightful lord. There was no prehistoric town in the little Trojan plain so garrisoned and provisioned as to withstand such a siege, nor could a host of a hundred thousand men have been supported in that open plain for even a single year.

Or, to descend to lesser details, who believes that the early Hellenes went forth to war beyond the seas provided with chariots and horses like Assyrian kings? Who supposes a pair of youths ever rode in such a chariot across the Peloponnese from Sphacteria to Sparta (Odyssey, III. 481; IV. 1), without even perceiving the inaccessible ridges of Taÿgetos that lie between?

In one of the earlier battles of the Iliad, two princes, diverse in race and, presumably, in speech, meet for the first time in the pitched battle under the walls of Troy. Within reach of each other's spears they chat in garrulous fashion, until they accidentally discover that their grandsires had once known each other as host and guest. They then strip off their armour and exchange it,—the Greek securing "gold for bronze, the value of a hundred oxen for the worth of nine,"—swear lifelong friendship, and agree to shun each other's spears in the fray (Iliad, VI. 119-236). Unless it be in the proportionate value of the metals in the Homeric age, or in the early tradition of Hellenic craft in barter,—still proverbial in the Levant,—what connection can be traced between any real or possible battle scene and such a poet's dream?

It is easy to continue this process of elimination, but it is *not* easy to arrive at any residuum which becomes historically certain, or even highly probable. Of course much in the Iliad is true to the poet's own time: but we can never sift it out. If there be any important exceptions to this statement, they will be found in passages generally regarded as late additions. Some of the civic and social scenes upon Achilles' shield (XVIII. 478–608) are realistic, whether the shield itself is a possible creation or not. Though the "Catalogue of Ships" represents truthfully no real armament, it is a pretty faithful list of the Greek cities then existing. But, even in such matters, we can usually reach little more than surmises.

It cannot even be shown that the legend was familiarly known and wide-spread among the Greek peoples, apart from its literary treatment by Homer. It is quite true that the setting of the story is a real earthly landscape, and a brief stay upon the shores of the Hellespont suffices to convince the pilgrim that the classic bard had himself visited the plain, and made good use of an excellent pair of eyes. I myself have beheld with delight the outspread panorama from Zeus' seat, on "the topmost peak of many-fountained Ida," and enjoyed the book of the Iliad read sitting beside " the fishy Hellespont," upon Achilles' tomb, — despite some misgivings lest we had selected the wrong mound. But so is the forest of Ardennes real; not, therefore, Orlando and Rosalind. Though some of us have doubtless visited Hamlet's castle, the royal ghost is still but a ghost. The site of Camelot may be identified; it will never be Tennyson's Camelot.

That some tradition of a real war formed the basis of the myth has been made more than probable by the important discoveries of Dr. Schliemann. Certainly at least one prehistoric city rich in gold existed in the Trojan plain, and was destroyed by fire. But any events which had occurred there came to the poet so refracted through an atmosphere of vague and fabulous tradition, that his work is in no wise hampered or limited by historic record or popular belief. The detailed story of Achilles' wrath is as clearly the conscious creation of a poetic mind as Prospero's enchanted island and its inhabitants.

That the general legend had been freely

treated by other poets before him, — just as
Tristram and Iseult are sung by Swinburne
and Tennyson and many another of earlier
days, — Homer himself plainly tells us.   He
introduces into the Odyssey minstrels of the
elder time, whose subjects are the Fate of
Ilios (Demodocos, VIII. 499 ff.) and the
Return of the Achaians (Phemios, I. 326).

The very dialect is a highly artificial and
copious one, created by long moulding in the
trough of the hexameter ; for it could never
have been spoken at any one time and
place.   Thus Homer uses freely *five* different forms for the infinitive verb "*be*"
(ἔμμεν, ἔμεν, ἔμμεναι, ἔμεναι, εἶναι), all of dif-
fering metrical value.   No one spoken dialect carries so many parallel forms at one
time.   Most of them, clearly, were archa-
isms even in the epic period.   This is but a
simple typical example.   Generations must
have laboured upon the heroic verse to ac-
cumulate such wealth of plastic materials.

The notion that Homer had anything of
the naïve simplicity usually attributed to
the popular ballad-maker is long since
abandoned.   Not merely by its magnificent

rhythm and Shakespearean wealth of vocabulary, but by its intensely dramatic situations, its abundance of ingenious and purely poetical detail, the Iliad is stamped unmistakably as a creation of consummate and self-conscious art. It certainly was the culmination of a long literary development: but was so successful that it has outlived the memory of its predecessors, and of the events which may have suggested them.

Homer, moreover, is careful to remind us often that even the princes and courts for whom he sings are nowise like the heroes of the epic song. The men of his own degenerate days could not lift Achilles' latch, nor Hector's stone, nor even old Nestor's drinking-bowl! One of the most prosaic passages is the so-called "Catalogue of Ships." Yet the singer here invokes anew the

Muses who dwell on Olympos,

and adds the humble confession : —

Only a rumour we hear, nor do we know anything surely.

Of the man Homer, and his life, also, we know nothing. All the discordant stories told of him by later Greeks stamp themselves plainly as feeble inventions. That he was a conscious artist was asserted just now simply because his works so declare him. All the minstrels and bards mentioned in the Homeric poems, — Thamyris, Demodocos, Phemios, and the rest, — are court poets, honoured of men and listened to with delight. That Homer himself wished, at least, to be heard and applauded by nobles and princes, is clear. His valorous men and fair women are all of lofty birth. Even the swineherd, who stands beside Odysseus so gallantly in the long fight with the suitors, was the son of a king in his own land, and is a slave and menial only through the fate of captivity (Od. XV. 403, etc.). One man of the people, only, Homer deigns to describe in detail, —and that one is the ridiculous Thersites. All this shows clearly how remote both poet and poem must have been from the free mercantile communities which we find in Asia Minor in the seventh century B.C., at the earliest dawn, that is, of authentic Greek history.

We said there was no evidence that the Trojan legend was a familiar one among Greeks generally before Homer glorified it. There are features in the construction of the Iliad indicating that it was unfamiliar to the poet's auditors. Opportunities are skilfully used, very early in the poem, to sketch in outline the essential features in the general tale of Troy. The birth and destiny of Achilles are touched upon in his appeal to his divine mother (I. 348, etc.). Helen's sin is mentioned (II. 161). The omens at Aulis before the fleet set sail, the duration and course of the war hitherto, are also impressively related within the first thousand lines (II. 301–332 and 134–138).

Moreover, there were a number of early Greek epics, younger, however, than Iliad or Odyssey, expressly intended to complete the " Epic Cycle " by relating events preceding, intervening between, and following the plots of the two greater poems. All but a few fragments perished long ago, but we chance to have a pretty full summary of their contents. Their length is also approximately known from the number of · books in each, these divisions being a mechanical convenience for rolling, not much older than the Alexandrian librarians.

Now, these "cyclic" epics were all comparatively brief. They were closely dependent on, in fact carefully dovetailed into, the two greater poems. They were chiefly occupied in elaborating and explaining allusions in the elder works. Where Homer was silent or ambiguous, *e.g.* as to the fate of leading characters like Æneas or Andromache, these later singers disagree hopelessly. They evidently did *not* draw heavily upon a mass of old and tenacious folk-lore which the Iliad (and Odyssey) had failed to exhaust. We think it is the prevailing belief of scholars, at present, that no such mass of Trojan legend existed, independent of the great literary epics.

The obvious but excellent comparison with the Arthur-cycle has been already suggested. Whether or not we cling fondly to our belief in a real Arthur, and Lancelot, and Merlin, we must see that any such reality has had little indeed to do with the evolution of the Tennysonian Idylls. A later English poet will count upon the presence of these Idylls, and very little else, in the memory of his audience.

The Homeric picture, then, stands practically isolated. Whatever historical details are truthfully given, we can never hope to select and verify them. Let us take a single important illustration : the question as to the age of Homer, the poet. The historical Greeks set at about two generations after Troy's fall the date for the great southward movement of the Dorian clans into the Peloponnese. This invasion was believed to have dethroned and expelled the great Achaian families, the posterity of Menelaos, Agamemnon, Nestor, and of the other chiefs familiar to us from the Iliad. The exiles of that age were supposed to have founded the Greek cities in Asia Minor. These traditions probably have a substantial basis of fact, and this temporary convulsion and retrogression in the Greek civilization may account in part for the great gap between Homeric life and customs, and those of later Greece. Did Homer, then, live before or after this upheaval?

Now, many of the ancients thought that Smyrna, the Greek city in Asia Minor, was pointed out by the weight of evidence as the birthplace of Homer; the modern students have quite largely agreed with them in this opinion. And yet, the poems themselves give no hint of any Greek cities existing, or destined to exist, in Asia at all! On the contrary, the poet is apparently quite unaware of this eastward colonizing movement, which is in truth the *first* great historical event in Greece which we can discern. It is not improbable that the siege of holy Ilios is in truth a far-off echo, or rather a sky-painted mirage, suggested merely by that stoutly resisted eastward colonization itself. But it can hardly be disproven, that Homer's life may actually have been spent *before* the final downfall of that brilliant Achaian civilization which he immortalizes in his poems. On this question Schuchhardt and Leaf disagree diametrically within one pair of covers.

It was the German scholar Welcker who first suggested that the gradual spread of interest in the epic school of poetry might be traced in the list of places claiming to be the birthplace of Homer. The most familiar form of this list is the one mentioned by Cicero, and forming a hexameter line : —

Smyrna, Chios, Colophon, Salamis, Rhodos,
Argos, Athenæ.

Numerous variations and substitutions were, however, current in antiquity. The mention of Chios in the lists is especially interesting, for the cause is probably to be found in the closing lines of the Homeric Hymn to Apollo, where the author, evidently describing himself, says, —

Blind is the man, and in Chios abounding
in crags is his dwelling.

The so-called Homeric hymns in honour of various divinities were attributed to Homer by the general voice of antiquity, and this very hymn to Apollo is so mentioned and quoted by Thucydides. As to the birthplace of the singer of the Iliad it is safer to be doubtful, but at least we may assert unhesitatingly that he was *not blind*, and not identical with the rather too self-conscious composer of this hymn to the Delian god.

But the more completely the tale of Troy, with its author, eludes the analysis of historian and archæologist, so much loftier is the position it assumes in its true character, as a masterpiece of imaginative poetry. The Iliad satisfies in large measure the three demands we may make upon any artistic creation: simplicity, truth, beauty. First, the plot is simple, its evolution complete, and its result inevitable. The subject announced in the opening line,

Sing, O goddess, the wrath of Achilles the offspring of Peleus,

is worked out — despite the somewhat protracted retardations and eddies in the story as we now have it — to its final results. Even the death of Achilles (XIX. 416–417 ; XXII. 359–360), and the fall of the guilty city (VI. 448–449 ; II. 329), are foreshadowed in so impressive a manner that all our reasonable curiosity is satisfied. Aristotle in his Poetics (§ 23) illustrates the unity of plot in the Iliad thus: "Only a single tragedy (or at most two) has been made out of either Iliad or Odyssey; but from the 'Little Iliad,'" (one of the brief continuations mentioned before) "more than eight," and *ten* are presently enumerated, if the text is sound. First, then, the story is a simple one.

Secondly, the warriors and matrons whom we see acting and suffering, whether real Greek men and women or not, are at any rate fully human. We do not demand that the conditions of their life shall be such as ever existed, or could have existed, on our earth. Nay, we escape gladly for the time being into the romantic and imaginative environment of the poet's scenes. But after all, it is not for angels nor for brutes, but only for men and women, that our warmest human interest can be aroused. And so we *do* demand, that within that environment Homer's people shall act as rational men and women would behave

c

under similar conditions ; or, at least, their actions must spring naturally from motives and impulses intelligible to us and adequate to arouse them. The tale then is not only simple, but truthful : *realistic*, if you like !

But thirdly, and chiefly, Homer's characters are heroic. They tower high above the commonplace levels of humanity. They are not so much like ourselves as what we would wish to become. Frankly, this seems to me the sole final test of the artist's right to be. We know the pettiness, the limitations, the disenchantments of life only too well. The artist is the creator of the beautiful. He must inspire and uplift us by setting before us something nobly simple and intelligible, wrought in our own divine likeness, but lovelier and loftier than our everyday selves.

It has been remarked already, that, while nominally dealing with a single episode in the last year of the long struggle, the Iliad alludes, in numerous passages, to events preceding and following. Still, many details of the larger myth, among them several which are now especially prominent and familiar, — Hecabè's dream, Paris' choice, Achilles' education as a girl, etc.—are to all appearances unknown to Homer, and due to the independent inventions of later poets and chroniclers. That almost any Greek mind would so assert its independence, is to be seen with singular clearness in the thousands of painted vases upon which familiar scenes from mythology and literature reappear. With few exceptions, even the mere artisans who devised these humble works of art introduced in each case more or less modifications, suited to their material and to the space at their command. Evidently the whole mass of myth long remained in a very plastic condition. This subject, however, has grown under the essayist's hand to a separate study, on the post-Homeric accretions to the myth (Ch. VII.).

The earliest link in the chain of woes distinctly mentioned by Homer is the elopement of Helen, Menelaos' wife and queen of Sparta, with the Trojan prince Paris or Alexandros. Though Achilles claims to have joined of his own free will, for justice's sake and glory's cause, in the expedition that avenged this crime, the other Greek chieftains may have been imagined as vassals, subject in some fashion to Menelaos and to his brother Agamemnon, lord of Mykenæ. Ten years have passed with little to mark their flight. The Greeks still lie encamped by the Hellespont, their vessels rotting on the shore.

The poem opens just after Achilles' sack of Thebè, identified by ancient geographers with a site on the southern foot-hills of Ida, in the fertile Adramyttian plain. A lovely captive maiden, Chryseïs, is assigned to Agamemnon. But she is the daughter of the priest of Apollo in his neighbouring shrine of Chrysè, and the god, hearkening to the father's prayers, sends upon the Greeks a deadly pestilence, which can be stayed only by the girl's release. Agamemnon reluctantly submits; but, stung by Achilles' taunts upon his greed and oppression, takes away instead, by force, Achilles' own beloved captive, Briseis, who would perhaps have been made the young hero's wife (Iliad, XIX. 295-299). Agamemnon thus commits, not even for love or passion's sake, but in mere tyrannous caprice, almost the very crime by which Paris has brought destruction on himself and all his folk. (Achilles remarks very effectively upon this when a reconciliation is first attempted. Iliad, IX. 335–343.)

Achilles now renounces the cause of the Atridæ, and retires to his cabin. Zeus promises Thetis signal vengeance on Agamemnon. Hector now ventures to sally forth into the plain with his garrison, and this entails many disasters for the Greeks.

This is of course the point in the legend which permitted large interpolation. The greater the efforts put forth to stay Hector, the more does their final failure glorify the Trojan hero, and possibly, through him, his conqueror, Achilles. But the exploits of other Greeks appealed, besides, to national, in some cases also to local, pride and patriotism. Diomedes, especially, in Book V., fairly outdoes Achilles, putting not only men to flight, but wounding both Aphrodite and Ares, the war-god himself. Most readers feel that the great protraction of these scenes mars the artistic form of the epic. In the course of a few days' fighting most of the Greek leaders are either slain or disabled. The chief pause in the midst of these tales of bloodshed is the ninth book, in which ambassadors from Agamemnon visit Achilles by night, and vainly implore him to relax his wrath. This scene is by many regarded also as the dividing line between the two great interpolations.

But finally Hector gains ground, until he actually sets fire to the Greek fleet. Achilles now reluctantly permits his beloved companion, the gentle Patroclos, to sally forth to aid his hard-pressed comrades-in-arms. Appearing in Achilles' armour, he is at first mistaken for the fleet-footed hero himself, and drives the panic-stricken Trojans before him. He is, however, himself finally overcome and slain by Hector. This is clearly an essential feature of the tale: and indeed, from this point events follow each other in rapid and inevitable succession.

The feud between Achilles and Agamemnon is now quickly stanched. Maddened by his friend's death, Pelides again takes the field. Clad in armour wrought for him, at Thetis' tearful request, by Hephaistos himself, the divine artificer, Achilles drives the men of Troy like sheep homeward. Last of all, though not without the aid of Pallas Athene in person, he slays in single combat the gallant Hector himself, who had ventured to tarry alone outside the walls and meet the onset of the resistless foeman. The action of Athene, however, in deceiving and disarming Hector, offends every Anglo-Saxon instinct for "fair play." It almost seems as if the poet himself (though he has just made Hector flee thrice in ignominious terror about the city wall) feels the same sympathy for the husband of Andromache that illumines the great family scene of parting in Book VI.

But we are many centuries yet before the age of chivalry. The Greek instinct preferred craft to force as frankly as does an American Indian. And, after all, the gods weight the scales for Hector's destruction because he is the bulwark of a lost, of an unrighteous cause. Achilles is to fare yet worse in death, falling without warning by

the hand of the cowardly and treacherous
Paris: — perhaps a just penalty for his
arrogance and cruelty.

For Troy is not to be taken by Achilles'
spear. His death, though it lies beyond
the frame of the Iliad itself, is clearly foreshadowed, being prophesied by his mother,
the lovely Nereid, who tells him : —

" Quickly for thee after Hector by fate thy
doom is appointed "

(Il. XVIII. 96.)

by the divine steed miraculously endowed
for this one utterance with mortal speech
(XIX. 416, 417), and still more plainly by
the expiring Hector (XXII. 359, 360), who
foretells for his slayer the approaching day,

". . . when Paris and Phœbus Apollo,
Valorous though thou art, at the Scæan
gate shall destroy thee."

The tale of Troy has in truth a charac-
teristically Greek conclusion, since the cunning of Odysseus is to succeed where the
martial prowess of all Achaia's chieftains
has failed.

With the single combat between Achilles and Hector, in the twenty-second book, the original Iliad may well have ended. It is precisely the point at which Virgil — a poet of most refined literary taste, at least — closes his imitative epic. The exact moment seems marked by the triumphant verses (XXII. 391–394): —

"Now, let us sing our pæan of Victory, sons of Achaia,
While to the ships we march, and with us carry the body ;
Great is the fame we have won : we have slain the illustrious Hector,
Him, who like to a god was implored in the town by the Trojans."

In fact, what immediately follows is not quite consistent with these lines, since Achilles alone drags Hector's body.

But the poet himself, or a disciple worthy to lift the enchanter's wand, perceived that the great epic should close amid calmer scenes, with an appeal to gentler emotions. In the twenty-third book is described the mourning for Patroclos, to which are added (partly, at least, by a late and feeble hand), the various games — archery, foot race, chariot contest, etc. — celebrated by Achilles about his friend's funeral mound.

The twenty-fourth book tells us how the savage Achilles himself is at last moved to desist from wrath and insult toward the dead, and to give up Hector's body for due funeral rites within the doomed city. In this culminating scene, the poet has ventured to bring together the two stateliest figures upon his broad canvas. The old King Priam, once the most prosperous monarch of Asia, now heavily burdened with years and sorrows, betakes himself to Achilles' encampment, and begs the privilege of ransoming the corpse of Hector, kissing as a suppliant the terrible hands which have bereft him of so many valiant sons !

Almost all students acquainted with the result of recent investigation, particularly in Germany, have abandoned, however reluctantly, the belief in one Homer, who created the Iliad in its present form, as literally as Dante composed the Commedia. Even Andrew Lang gives ground a bit, though in true Parthian fashion. On the other hand, there is hardly to be found nowadays a scholar who accepts the ballad-theory of Lachmann, who argued that our Iliad was pieced together in semi-mechanical fashion, at a late date, from many short lays originally disconnected with each other.

It is highly probable that the subject announced in the first line was worked out in a comparatively direct manner in a sustained epic poem, the nucleus of the present one, and perhaps one-third or one-fourth as long, to its natural conclusion, namely, the death of Hector. Whether so named or not, this was an Achilleid, as Grote calls it. But so many episodes were subsequently inserted, — some of them, perhaps, by the original poet, — that the book we now read is not merely the tale of Achilles' wrath, but more nearly suits its actual title, the Iliad; that is, the story of Ilios, or Troy. Still, nearly every one of these additions, large and small, must have been composed expressly for the place which it occupies. Each part was fitted into the artistic whole, though they were not all shaped by the same artist's hand. (This is, in general terms, the theory of Von Christ, of Leaf, of Jebb, — and perhaps of classical students generally. Mathematical proof, or even argument in details, is impossible, from the nature of the case. The attempt of Professor Jebb, in the fourth chapter of his indispensable Introduction to Homer, to distinguish the successive strata almost line by line, is as temperate and scholarly as any such undertaking can be. If he were to re-edit it once a year, however, he would inevitably disagree with himself in every fresh edition.)

The noble twenty-fourth book, indeed, is not even an insertion, but a continuation of the story beyond the limit announced at the beginning. It is probably not from the original composer's hand ; but we need not hesitate to declare that it lifts the whole tale to a nobler and gentler plane of feeling, — and for that very reason is perhaps more likely to be the expression of the ideals of a later and more refined generation.   In ethical tone it resembles the Odyssey rather than the older portions of the Iliad.

There may seem at first to be an inconsistency in the views here set forth ; but, in fact, unity of design in a great work of art does not necessarily indicate unity of authorship.   There is one analogy, at least, so obvious that the thought which rises in the writer's mind is, doubtless, a mere reminiscence of others' words.   A stranger wandering through a great mediæval cathedral, or, let us say, Westminster Abbey, might well be struck by the harmonious design which dominates all the variations in detail.   On reaching the chapel of Henry the Seventh, he might very naturally exclaim: "This is in truth the soul and key to the whole structure!   This portion, surely, is from the very hand of the original artist who planned the noble building."   A similar expression might rise to the lips of a lover of literature, as he arrives at this culminating scene of the Iliad.   The artistic instincts of both are right.   The conclusions may be equally wrong.

But the question " Who constructed it? " is, after all, a secondary problem, and, perhaps, an insoluble one, in both cases. Even in Seneca's day, those who hoped to solve the Homeric question were recognized as a special class of harmless madmen! Let us, at least, learn to say, with Emerson : —

> Beauty into my senses stole.
> I yielded myself to the perfect whole.

Even Wolf, the first great assailant of the single authorship of the Iliad, relates how he became indignant at his own doubts, as often as he gave himself up to the golden spell of the epic story, that sweeps on like a majestic river moving resistless to the sea. (Cf. Jebb, Introduction to Homer, p. 110.)

II

WOMANHOOD IN THE ILIAD

THE Iliad offers us the oldest picture which we have of the life of man on the continent of Europe. This picture is also a most vivid and beautiful one. There is a constant temptation, therefore, to treat the poem as a starting-point and substantial basis for the history of our civilization. Any attempt of this kind, however, seems, as has been indicated, almost utterly vain and elusive. Before we undertake to recover, by sifting the materials at our command, the true picture of Homeric manners, customs, and beliefs, let us seriously imagine Macaulay's New Zealander, three thousand years hence, employed in reconstructing England as it was under the Tudors, with no materials save the Faery Queen and Chaucer's Knight's Tale. Or,

31

to match the Theogony and Works and Days of Hesiod, let him be furnished with Pilgrim's Progress and Snowbound. Instead of the fragments of the Greek lyric poets, we may generously permit Andrew Lang's Blue Book of Poetry to drift down intact. We should still fail to recognize our kinsfolk in the picture he would draw.

Perhaps, however, our feeling can be better illustrated by a figure. A traveller, crossing the Alps by rail at night, may be awakened by a peal of thunder, and, pushing aside his curtains, sees, perchance, across a wide intervale, a panorama of stately mountains, their outlines half shrouded in storm-clouds. The scene is illuminated for a single instant by the unearthly glare of the lightning. The next second he falls back into dreamless slumber. In the morning, indeed for life, that picture abides with him : whether in memory or in imagination he hardly knows, but certainly little associated, if at all, with the scenes, whatever they may be, that greet him in the familiar light of the sun. The pilgrim is the Western Aryan. The vision of the night is the Homeric age. The real dawn of our historical knowledge, the awakening of the race, as it were, to its own continuous life, lies not far behind the first historian, Herodotus, who lived in the fifth century before our era. Even to him, the men his grandsires knew — gentle Crœsus and ruthless Cyrus, Solon the wise and Polycrates the fortunate — stand with blurred outlines against a background of fable : dim gigantic shapes in the mists of morning.

How long before himself the poet Homer had lived Herodotus can only conjecture, and his conjecture is, four centuries, — just the gap that yawns to-day between us and Columbus. And think what impenetrable mystery would now enshroud the figure of the Genoese adventurer, had his age transmitted to us, through generations utterly destitute of historical records, nothing save a metrical romance !

But even Homer, or, let us say, the Homeric poets, avowedly described, not their own ignobler days, but a more heroic, far-distant foretime whereof they

D

> Hear but the rumour alone, and know
> nothing as certain.

Brilliant as is the fabric of this vision, it is inextricably interwoven with the super-human and the marvellous. If we attempt to strip Achilles of his divine armour, bid his immortal steed be mute, deny him the sea-nymph for a mother, — hero and lay alike will soon crumble away under our impious hands! Over all parts of the picture alike there lies the light that never was on sea or land, the glow of poetic imagination.

It is thus that we should receive and read the tale. It remains none the less true, — not to mere authentic dates and historical events, but in a higher sense, like the Dantesque Purgatorio, or Prospero's enchanted isle, true to the eternal laws of artistic creation, and to the cravings of baffled, weary humanity, reaching forth eagerly after the higher truthfulness of perfect beauty.

We do not present here, then, the first chapter of an historical essay upon the development of woman. How far the social conditions of Homeric Troy, and of the Iliad generally, represent the observation of the poet at any particular place and time can never be known. We desire merely to unroll a few of the quieter scenes in the lurid panorama of the Iliad. The translator is, for his own part, fully assured that we gaze, through the poet's eyes, upon a glorified vision of men and women as they might have been. Even while our tears fall with theirs, we see in Hector and Andromache not the features of any one loving pair that ever lived and died, but rather immortal types of an idealized humanity. We shall expect, therefore, to find in the women of Homer, as in his heroes, not highly individualized characters, hardly even specifically Greek figures, but rather natures simply human, swayed by the strongest and most universal passions and motives. Andromache, the Cilician wife of a Trojan prince, immortalized in the verses of a Greek poet, is herself neither a Greek, a Trojan, nor a Cilician. She stands upon a pedestal, and we look up reverently to the inspired creation of a master artist.

On the Greek side, to be sure, the Iliad presents for the most part only the lawless social conditions of a permanent camp. Yet even here we are not left without reminders that women are indispensable to the happier side of life. The very absence of the Achaians from their own firesides, through so many darkening years, is an element of pathos, to which the poet has appealed in memorable passages.

"Whoso tarries afar from his wife, in a
    many-oared vessel,
One month only, is chafed in spirit, so long
    as the gusty
Storms of the winter and furious water
    detain him from sailing.
But for ourselves in the ninth year passing,
    as here we have lingered."

                (Il. II. 292–296.)

Several times also, amid the wild turmoil of war, an effective simile suddenly transports us to scenes of peaceful life, and even of humble toil. Thus the equal poise of a well-contested fight is illustrated by the figure of a woman

Holding the scales, who raises the wool and
    the weights together,

Balancing them, to win scant wage for her-
    self and her children.

                 (Il. XII. 434, 435.)

Still more striking by its unexpected tender-
ness is the picture that is called up by
Achilles, as he reproves his friend for
shedding tears over the disasters of the
Greeks : —

" Why do you weep, O Patroclos ?   E'en
    as a fond little maiden,
Running beside her mother, and begging
    the mother to take her,
Plucking her still by the gown, and striving
    from haste to detain her,
Tearfully looks in her face, until she indeed
    is uplifted, —
Like unto her, O Patroclos, the swelling
    tears you are shedding ! "

                 (Il. XVI. 7–11.)

There are, moreover, some women in the
Greek camp itself. The pathos of their
fate is evidently felt by the poet. They are
for the most part the sole survivors from
the lesser towns of the Troad, which have
been successively stormed and sacked by
Achilles. They have lost, at a single blow,

kindred, home, freedom, often honour as well. Of these unhappy creatures we have occasional vivid glimpses, and two of their number stand forth with distinctness, — are indeed essential to the epic plot.

Fair-cheeked Chryseis, a less tragic figure than the rest, merely glides like a swift vision of maidenhood through the opening scenes of the tale. She is not left friendless nor forsaken, for her kindred were not with her when she fell into captivity. How it chanced that this girl, who dwelt with her father, Apollo's priest, in holy Chrysè, was taken in Andromache's town, Thebè, Homer does not pause to explain. The poem opens with her father's plea for her release, Agamemnon's scornful refusal, the prayer of Chryses to the god he served, and Apollo's response. When the angry sun-god sends a pestilence upon the host, Agamemnon's stubborn heart yields, like Pharaoh's. So Chryseis' day of captivity is brief, and seemingly not bitter. Her release is the first and pleasantest result of the stormy council of Greek chieftains. Before the first rhapsody closes, the glancing-eyed maiden trips lightly upon Odysseus' ship for the homeward voyage. It is apparently only a few hours later, when she is placed in her father's arms, who

> rejoicing,
> Welcomed his daughter beloved.
>
> (Il. I. 446, 447.)

There is a powerful tribute to her beauty, — and a dark hint of the fate from which she was rescued, the fate of Cassandra not long afterward, — in the expression which Agamemnon had made of his reluctance to give her up : —

> "I am greatly desirous
> In my household to keep her; I prize her
>   above Clytemnestra,
> Who is my lawful wife; nor is she inferior
>   to her,
> Either in stature or beauty, in cunning of
>   mind or of body."
>
> (Il. I. 112–115.)

If Chryseis' youth was troubled with other sorrows, they probably did not arise from the presence of the Grecian host, who had well learned in her case the lesson of "wisdom through suffering."

Briseis' fate is more closely entangled with the darkest threads of the tragic drama. At her first appearance, indeed, she is a mere silhouette, as she passes reluctantly down the strand from Achilles' cabin, led by the heralds to the galley of Agamemnon, who has ruthlessly claimed her to make good his loss. The leading away of Briseis is represented more than once upon Greek vases, and is also the subject of one of the largest and finest Pompeian wall-paintings. The face of Achilles is in itself a poem. (See Baumeister, p. 723.)

The event was evidently regarded as the decisive point in the quarrel between the leaders. It is this seizure of his favourite that stirs Achilles' wrath so deeply that he holds aloof from the war. When Agamemnon, after the first series of disasters, sends the ineffectual embassy to Achilles (in the ninth book), he not only offers many royal gifts, but also proposes to restore Briseis, and declares that he himself has shown her no discourtesy during her enforced stay under his roof. When she actually returns, after the reconciliation between the quar-

relling chiefs, it is to find the gentle Patroclos dead in the cabin which she had shared,
we know not how long, with the illustrious
pair of friends and her fellow-captives.   In
her instant lament over him, not only do
we hear nearly all we shall ever learn of
her own piteous story, but there also comes
into view a peculiarly winning and amiable
side of the dead hero's character.

Then Briseis, as lovely as Aphrodite the
        golden,
When she beheld Patroclos, so mangled by
        keen-edged weapons,
Throwing her arms about him, lamented
        shrill, with her own hands
Tearing her shapely neck, her breast, and
        her glorious features.
Then the divinely beautiful woman bewailed
        and addressed him :
"O thou dearest of men to my hapless
        spirit, Patroclos,
Living I left thee here when I from the
        cabin departed ;
Dead do I find thee now at my coming, O
        chief of the people !
So evermore upon me comes sorrow close
        upon sorrow.

Him upon whom my father and mother
    bestowed me, my husband,
Saw I mangled with keen-edged spears, in
    defence of his city.
Then, though Achilles the swift, when he
    ravaged the city of Mynes,
Slew my husband in battle, yet thou for-
    badst me to sorrow,
Promising I should become the wife of the
    godlike Achilles :
He, thou saidst, would lead me with him
    on the vessels to Phthia ;
There in the midst of his folk would my
    marriage feast be appointed.
Therefore I mourn for thee dead, who living
    ever wast gentle."
Weeping so did she speak, and in answer
    lamented the women,
As for Patroclos they moaned : yet *her own
    woes each was bewailing.*

(Il. XIX. 282–300.)

We cannot refrain from calling attention
to that closing phrase, with its quiet touch
of sympathy.

A last glimpse of Briseis tells us only
that she regained the position of Achilles'
favourite, held during her absence by a Les-
bian captive, " fair-cheeked Diomedè." It

is in that magnificent final act of the drama,
when the suppliant king in the cabin of his
foe, utterly exhausted by vigils and fasting,
is forced to give way to sleep. A couch is
spread for Priam under the portico, and

Meantime Achilles also slept, in the well-
    built cabin's
Inner recess, and beside him was lying the
    lovely Briseis.

(Il. XXIV. 675, 676.)

The first woman, however, to appear
prominently in the Iliad is, fitly enough,
Helen herself, the source of all the woes of
Troy. Though she is under the especial
charge of Aphrodite, and is once called
Zeus' daughter, Helen seems to be, in the
Iliad, merely a fair, selfish, fickle woman.
The marvellous and superhuman elements in
her nature and destiny are, apparently, later
additions to the tale. We have mentioned
that the carrying off of Helen by the roving
Paris is the first link in the chain of evil
with which Homer is acquainted. Her own
sin is, perhaps, confined to a later acquiescence in their union, and a fondness for

Paris which has now largely passed away. She has already been twenty years in Ilios.

In the third book of the Iliad Helen is summoned from the palace of her lover by the tidings that he and Menelaos are to contend in single combat for the possession of herself and the treasures stolen with her. Perhaps her lack of deeper feeling is hinted at by the manner in which the messenger finds her employed.

> A magnificent web she was weaving,
> Twofold, purple in colour, and thereon she
>   had embroidered
> Many a battle of knightly Trojans and
>   mailèd Achaians,
> Fought for the sake of herself, and under
>   the hands of Ares.
>
> (Il. III. 125–128.)

For whom the single tear falls, as she leaves her loom, Homer does not tell: it may be he — or even she — did not know. Save for an occasional epithet, usually " trailing-robed," no attempt is made to indicate her beauty. Instead, the old men, looking down, from the tower over the gate, upon panic-stricken city, devastated fields, and beleaguering hosts, murmur at her approach : —

"Nowise marvellous is it that Trojans and
    mailèd Achaians,
Over a woman like this, through the long
    years suffer in sorrow:
Wondrous like to the deathless goddesses is
    she in beauty."

(Ibid. 156–158.)

But of course the sober second thought of
age quickly follows,

"Yet even so, though lovely she be, let her
    fare in the vessels ;
Let her not leave vexation behind her for
    us and our children."

(Ibid. 159, 160.)

Priam greets Helen with the courtesy of a
king, saying, among other things : —

"Nowise guilty I hold you ; the gods are
    responsible only,
Who have incited against me the fatal war
    of the Argives."

(Ibid. 164, 165.)

After a few words of self-abasement, she
points out, at the aged monarch's request,

the Hellenic chieftains in the plain below. The loneliness of her life in Troy, cut off from her race and kin, is brought out, but with no undue emphasis, in the passage concerning her brothers; which incidentally confirms our belief that to the poet of the Iliad Helen and her brothers are mortal, and of merely human nature. It is more prudent to quote here the deservedly famous and oft-cited version of Dr. Hawtrey. It is Helen who speaks: —

"Clearly the rest I behold of the dark-eyed
    sons of Achaia ;
Known to me well are the faces of all ; their
    names I remember ;
Two, two only remain, whom I see not
    among the commanders, —
Kastor fleet in the car, Polydeukes brave
    with the cestus ;
Own dear brethren of mine ; one parent
    loved us as infants.
Are they not here in the host, from the
    shores of loved Lakedaimon,
Or, though they came with the rest in ships
    that bound through the waters,
Dare they not enter the fight or stand in the
    council of heroes,

All for fear of the shame and the taunts my
    crime has awakened?"
So said she. They long since in Earth's
    soft arms were reposing,
There in their own dear land, their father-
    land, Lakedaimon.

(Il. III. 234-244.)

The combat ends with Paris' discomfiture,
and Aphrodite has to interfere and snatch
him away in a cloud to save his forfeit life;
but there is nothing to indicate that Helen
is more concerned than any other spectator.
Then Aphrodite appears to Helen in the
guise of an old woman, and bids her return
home to console her lover. Helen refuses
with pettish rudeness, bidding Aphrodite go
to him herself, "to become his wife, or his
handmaid." Her chief concern is for her
own disgrace.

> "The Trojan women behind me
> All will jeer, and I in spirit have sorrows
>   unnumbered."

(*Ibid.* 411, 412.)

Yet to a second and sterner summons she
renders prompt obedience. Perhaps the
goddess only stands for the lawless love

in Helen's own breast. At least, there is often a temptation to have recourse to such allegorical interpretations, when a divinity appears only to a single person, and merely for a moment. So, in the council scene already mentioned, Pallas darts from heaven to bid Achilles refrain from physical violence against Agamemnon. She is revealed only to the son of Peleus, and seems little more than his own wiser self, his sober second thought.

Upon reaching the chamber of Paris, Helen taunts him with his overthrow, but she is unable to resist his wheedling words, and is presently only too ready to accept his caresses. There is no moment when the doom of Troy seems so imminent, and so deserved, as at the close of the third book, when we see, as it were, at the same glance, the guilty lovers in their momentary security, and Menelaos, raging like a baffled lion up and down the place of combat, hoping yet to discover and slay his vanquished enemy. The poet adds, grimly, that not one of the Trojans would have screened their prince, but would gladly have pointed him out to the injured husband, "for he was hated like black death by them all."

We are now approaching the chief series of home and domestic scenes in the poem, the episode for the sake of which any paper like the present is largely written. There is the less objection to detaching Hector's visit to Troy from its present connection in the poem, because it can hardly have been composed for the place it now occupies. It is not like Hector to leave a desperate and losing fight that he may take a message to the city, — which any page could have carried as well as he, — and to linger there for an hour at least, forgetful of his duties as commander in the field. The pathos of the immortal parting scene is materially lessened, also, as we discover that Hector, for two succeeding nights, came back in safety to Andromache's arms, encamped on the third and fourth nights in the plain, and perished only on the fifth day !

The episode of his visit to Ilios fills the greater part of the sixth book. Diomedes has more than taken Achilles' place during

E

the first day's fighting, putting men and gods to rout. In the midst of the flight and panic of the Trojans, Helenos, their chief priest and seer, bids his brother Hector, first rallying and ordering the terrified host, go straightway to the city. He must command Hecabè, the queen, to assemble the aged women of Troy and to go in procession to Pallas Athene's temple with a propitiatory offering. Little actually occurs during his absence. The poet fills the gap by recording the famous dialogue between Diomedes and Glaucos, with their exchange of armour on the battle-field.

It would be impertinent to interrupt the unbroken flow of the famous rhapsody with any extended comment or discussion. We must venture, however, to call the reader's attention beforehand to the skilful use that is made of golden silence in this part of the poem; to Hector as he receives with unuttered scorn Paris' voluble excuses; to Andromache, who is already departed, a tear in her eye and a smile on her lip, toward her desolate home, ere Hec-

tor's last words are uttered ; but, above
all, to the eloquent muteness of Hecabè,
lady of many sorrows, turning away obediently to do the bidding of her valorous
and dutiful son, who has just prayed
with all his heart for the speedy death
of the guilty, selfish, best-belovèd younger
brother !

(HECTOR'S VISIT TO ILIOS.)

When now Hector arrived at the Scæan
    gate and the beech-tree,
Round him quickly were gathered the daugh-
    ters and wives of the Trojans,
Asking for news of their friends, — of child
    and brother and husband.
Hector commanded them unto the gods to
    make their petition,
All of them, each in her turn ; but grief
    was appointed for many.

Presently he was arrived at the beautiful
    palace of Priam.
It was adorned with porches of polished
    columns.   Within it
Chambers, fifty in number, of shining mar-
    ble were builded ;
Close at the side of each other they stood ;
    and there did the princes

Dwell with their lawful wives.   On the in-
    nermost side of the courtyard,
Opposite, stood the abode of the married
    daughters of Priam,
Twelve roofed chambers of shining marble,
    and close to each other.
There had the daughters of Priam their
    home, with the men they had wedded.

There his bountiful mother came forth to
    receive him, and with her
Led she Laodike, who was the fairest in
    face of her daughters.
Closely she clung to his hand, and thus in
    words she addressed him :
"Child, why is it you come, deserting the
    furious combat ?
Hard pressed surely are ye by the hateful
    sons of the Argives
Struggling about our town ; and your own
    spirit has brought you
Hither, to lift your hands unto Zeus from
    the heights of the city.
Yet pray wait till I bring you the wine that
    is sweeter than honey ;
So you may pour a libation to Zeus and the
    other immortals
First, and then 'twere well for you your-
    self if you quaffed it.

Mightily wine increases the strength of a
    man exhausted,
Even as you are exhausted by strife in de-
    fence of your dear ones.''

(Homer often, as Horace says, ''confesses
his fondness for wine by singing its praises.''
This passage, however, enforces rather the
need of temperance, as will quickly appear.)

Then unto her made answer the great
    bright-helmeted Hector:
'' Proffer me not the delightsome wine, O
    reverend mother,
Lest you enfeeble my limbs, and my force
    and my strength be forgotten.
Yet uncleansed are my hands. I fear me
    to pour in libation
Gleaming wine unto Zeus. To the cloud-
    wrapt monarch of heaven
I, who with gore am beflecked, may dare
    not to make my petition.
But do you go yourself to the fane of Athene
    the Spoiler;
Gather the aged dames, and carry your of-
    ferings with you.
Ay, and a robe in your hall that is lying,
    the fairest and largest,
Dearest of all to your heart, you shall also
    bear to the temple.

Lay this over the knees of the fair-tressed
    goddess Athene.
Promise her, too, you will slay twelve oxen
    for her in the temple,
Sleek, that know not the goad, if she will
    have pity upon you,
Saving the Trojans' wives, their helpless
    children, and city,
If she afar from sacred Troy will hold
    Diomedes,
That undaunted spearman, the savage, the
    rouser of terror.
So do you go your ways to the fane of
    Athene the Spoiler;
I myself am going to seek and to call Alex-
    andros,
If he perchance be willing to heed me.
    Yet were it better
Earth should yawn for him! Truly the
    lord of Olympus has made him
Source of woe unto Troy, and to Priam the
    brave and his children.
Gladly indeed unto Hades' gate would I see
    him descending:
Then would I say that my heart had a joy-
    less sorrow forgotten."

So did he speak; but the mother returned
    to her home, and commanded

Straightway her maids, who assembled the
    aged dames of the city.
Hecabè down to her odorous treasure-cham-
    ber descended ;
There were the garments richly embroidered,
    the labour of women,
Wrought by Sidonian women, whom Alex-
    ander the godlike
Brought from Sidon with him, as the wide-
    wayed water he traversed,
Homeward sailing to Troy with Helena
    daughter of princes.
One robe Hecabè lifted, and brought as a
    gift to Athene :
This was the one of them all most fairly
    embroidered and largest ;
Brightly it shone as a star, and under the
    rest it was lying.
Forth she fared, and the ancient dames in
    multitude followed.

When they were come to Athene's fane
    on the heights of the city,
She of the beautiful cheeks, Theano the
    daughter of Kisseus, —
She who was wife to the knightly Antenor,
    — opened the portal,
Since she had been of the Trojans appointed
    Athene's priestess.

They, with a prayerful wail, all raised their
    hands to Athene,
While bright-faced Theano uplifted the robe
    and bestowed it
Over the knees of the fair-tressed goddess
    Athene; and loudly
Unto the daughter of Zeus supreme she
    made her petition.
  " Royal Athene, the saver of towns, O
    goddess divinest,
Break, I pray, Diomedes' lance, and grant
    that the hero
Prone in the dust shall lie, at the Scæan
    gate of the city.
So that to thee straightway twelve kine we
    will slay in thy temple,
Sleek, that know not the goad, if thou wilt
    have pity upon us,
Saving the Trojans' wives, their helpless
    children, and city."
Thus she prayed:—but Athene tossed her
    head in refusal.

(This gesture is still perfectly natural to
every Greek.)

While to the daughter of Zeus most high
    they made their petition,
Hector had come meantime to the beautiful
    palace of Paris;

This Alexander himself had built, with the
    craftiest workmen, —
Best of the builders were they in the fertile
    land of the Troad, —
Near unto Priam's and Hector's home, on
    the heights of the city.
Hector, beloved of Zeus, passed into the
    palace, and with him
Carried his spear, full six yards long; and
    brightly before him
Glittered the point of bronze, and the golden
    circlet upon it.
Paris he found in his chamber, preparing
    his beautiful armour,
Shield and breastplate, and testing his
    bended bow and his arrows.
Argive Helen was sitting among her women
    attendants.
Glorious works of the loom her maidens
    wrought at her bidding.
  Hector reproached his brother in words
    of scorn as he saw him:
" Sirrah, it is not well to cherish your anger
    within you.
Perishing now are the people about our city
    and rampart,
Waging the strife; but for your sake only
    the battle and war-cry
Rages around our town; and you would be
    wroth with another,

If you should find him skulking afar from
    the hateful encounter.
Up, then, ere our homes with devouring
    flames shall be kindled!"

  Then, in reply to his brother, thus spake
    Alexander the godlike:
"Hector, indeed you reproach me with
    justice, no more than I merit.
Therefore to you will I speak, and do you
    give attention and hearken.
Not out of rage at the Trojans so much, nor
    yet in resentment
Here in my chamber I sate, but I wished to
    give way to my sorrow.
Yet even now my wife, with gentle entreaty
    consoling,
Bade me go forth to the fray, and I, too,
    think it is better.
Victory comes unto this one in turn, and
    again to another.
Tarry a moment, I pray, till I don mine
    armour for battle;
Or, do you go, and I will pursue, and, I
    think, overtake you."
  So did he speak; and to him bright-
    helmeted Hector replied not.
Helen, however, with gentlest accents spoke
    and addressed him.

"Brother of mine, — of a wretch, of a
    worker of evil, a horror !
Would that the selfsame day whereon my
    mother had borne me,
I had been seized and swept by the furious
    breath of the storm-wind
Into the mountains, or else to the sea with
    its thundering billows.
There had I met my doom, ere yet these
    deeds were accomplished !
Or, as the gods had appointed for me this
    destiny wretched,
Truly I wish I had been with a man more
    valorous wedded,
Who would have heeded the scorn of the
    folk and their bitter resentment.
Never a steadfast spirit in this man abides,
    nor will it
Ever hereafter be found ; and methinks his
    reward will be ready ! —
Nay, but I pray you to enter, and here on
    a chair to be seated,
Brother, for on your heart most heavily laid
    is the burden
Wrought by my own base deeds and the
    sinful madness of Paris.
Evil the destiny surely that Zeus for us
    twain has appointed,
Doomed to be subjects of song among men
    of a far generation."

Then unto her made answer the great
    bright-helmeted Hector:
" Helena, bid me not sit, — nor will you,
    tho' gracious, persuade me.
Eagerly yearns my spirit to fight in defence
    of the Trojans,
While among them there is longing already
    for me in my absence.
This one I pray you to rouse, and let him
    make haste for himself, too,
So he may yet overtake me before I depart
    from the city,
Since I am now on my way to my home, in
    the hope I may find there
Both my wife and my infant son, and the
    rest of my household :
For if again I may come returning in safety
    I know not,
Or if already the gods by the hands of
    Achaians shall slay me.''

He, so speaking, departed, — the great
    bright-helmeted Hector.
Presently into his own well-builded palace
    he entered.
Yet his wife, white-armed Andromache, was
    not within it.
She with her infant child and her fair-robed
    maid had departed.

Now on the tower at the gate she stood, and
bewailed and lamented.
Hector, when he had found not the blame-
less lady within doors,
Came and stood at the threshold, and thus
did he speak to his servants :
"Tell me, I pray you, O serving-maidens,
the truth with exactness.
Whither is lovely Andromache out of her
palace departed ?
Is she then gone to the home of my brothers'
wives, or my sisters',
Or did she fare to the shrine of the goddess
Athene, where others,
Fair-tressed Trojan dames, are appeasing
the terrible goddess ? "
Then made answer to him their faithful
housekeeper, saying :
"Hector, since you have bidden us tell you
the truth with exactness,
Not to your sisters' home, nor your brothers'
wives' she departed,
Nor did she go to the shrine of the goddess
Athene, where others,
Fair-tressed Trojan dames, are appeasing
the terrible goddess.
But to the tower of Ilios sped she, since it
was told her
Hard were the Trojans prest, and great was
the might of the Argives.

Therefore she in her eager haste has rushed
   to the rampart
Like one crazed; and the nurse, with the
   boy in her arms, went also.''
  So did the servant reply, and Hector
   rushed from the palace,
Back by the well-built ways, and the path
   he so lately had traversed.
So through the city he passed, and came to
   the Scæan gateway,
Where he intended forth to the plain and
   the battle to sally.
There did his bounteous wife, Andromache,
   running to meet him
Come, — Andromache, child of Eëtion, fear-
   less in spirit.
He, Eëtion, dwelt at the foot of deep-wooded
   Plakos;
Ruled the Cilician folk in Thebè under the
   mountain.
She was his daughter, and wife unto brazen-
   helmeted Hector.
So she came and met him, and with her fol-
   lowed the servant,
Clasping the innocent boy to her bosom, —
   yet but an infant,
Hector's well-loved child, — and brightly he
   shone as a star shines.
Hector Scamandrios called him, the others
   Astyanax named him,

— Prince of the city, — for Hector alone
    was Ilios' bulwark.

(Hector is too modest to call his child
Lord of the Town, and names him instead
Child of our River. Some commentators
have cut out these lines as *unpoetical*.)

    Smiling the father stood, as he looked at
       his son, and in silence.
Close to his side, with a tear in her eye,
       Andromache, pressing,
Clung to her husband's hand, and thus she
       spoke and addressed him :
    " Ah me, surely your prowess will slay
       you ! Nor will you have pity,
Not for your helpless child, nor yet for my-
       self the ill-fated.
Soon I of you shall be robbed. Ere long the
       Achaians will slay you,
All of them rushing upon you ! And truly,
       for me it were better,
When I of you am bereft, to go down to the
       grave. Nor hereafter
May consolation be mine, when once your
       doom is accomplished,
Only laments ! No father have I, nor rever-
       end mother.
Well do you know how godlike Achilles
       murdered my father,

When he had sacked our city, that well-
    built town of Cilicians,
Thebè with lofty gates ; and Eëtion also he
    murdered,
Though he despoiled him not, since that he
    dreaded in spirit.
There did the victor burn his body, in beau-
    tiful armour.
He, too, heaped up a mound ; and the elms
    are growing about it,
Set by the Oreads, sprung from Zeus, who
    is lord of the ægis.
Seven my brethren were, who together abode
    in the palace.
All on a single day passed down to the
    dwelling of Hades,
Each of them slain by the sword of the fleet-
    footed, godlike Achilles, —
They, and the white-fleeced sheep, and the
    herds of slow-paced oxen.

(There is something peculiarly tender in
the wistful memory which recalled these
humbler victims, that had shared in the
general wreck of the happy pastoral life.)

Lastly, my mother, who ruled as queen
    under deep-wooded Plakos :
Though he had led her hither along with
    the rest of his booty,

Yet he released her again, and accepted a
    bountiful ransom.
Then, in the hall of her father, the huntress
    Artemis slew her.

(That is, she died a sudden and painless
death.)

Hector, so you are to me both father and
    reverend mother;
You are my brother as well, and you are
    my glorious husband.
Pray have pity upon me, and tarry you here
    on the rampart,
Lest you may leave as an orphan your boy,
    and your wife as a widow.
Order your people to stand by the fig-tree,
    since upon that side
Easier gained is the wall, and exposed to
    assault is the city.
(Certainly thrice already the bravest have
    come to attempt it:
Ajax the less and the greater, renowned
    Idomeneus with them,
Tydeus' valorous son, and both of the chil-
    dren of Atreus.
Whether because some man well skilled in
    augury bade them,
Or it may chance that their own hearts
    urged and impelled them to do it.")

F

Then unto her made answer the great
bright-helmeted Hector :
" Surely for all these things, my wife, am
I troubled, but greatly
Shamed were I before Trojans and long-
robed Trojan matrons,
If like a coward I lingered afar from the
war and the battle.
Nor has my heart so bade me, because I
have learned to be always
Valiant and ready to fight in the foremost
line of our people,
Striving to win high fame, for myself and
for Priam my father.
This, too, well do I know, — in my heart
and my soul it abideth :
Surely a day shall come when the sacred city
shall perish,
Priam himself, and the folk of Priam the
valorous spearman.
Yet far less do I grieve for the Trojans' sorrows hereafter,
Even the woes of Hecabè's self, and of Priam
the monarch,
Or for the fate of my brethren, though many
will perish undaunted,
Falling prone in the dust by the hands of the
merciless foemen, —
Less do I grieve for all this than for you,
when a warrior Achaian

Leads you lamenting away, for the day of
    your freedom is ended.
Then as another's slave at the loom you will
    labour in Argos,
Or from the spring Hypereia draw water, or
    else from Messeis,
Oft in reluctance, because compulsion is
    heavy upon you.
Then, as you weep, perchance 'twill be said
    by one who shall see you,
'Yon is Hector's wife, who still among
    knightly Trojans
Bravest proved in the fray, when Troy was
    with battle encircled.'
So some day they will speak, and again will
    the pain be repeated,
Since of so faithful a husband bereft you
    suffer in bondage.
Verily dead may I be, and the earth heaped
    heavy upon me,
Ere I may hear thy cry, or behold thee
    dragged by the foemen."

Speaking thus, for his son reached out the
    illustrious Hector ;
Yet he backward recoiled on the breast of
    the faithful attendant,
Crying aloud in his fright at the sight of
    his father belovèd.

'Twas by the brazen mail and the horse-
    hair plume he was frightened,
Seeing it nodding so fiercely adown from
    the crest of his helmet.
Then out laughed the affectionate father
    and reverend mother.
Presently now the illustrious Hector lifted
    his helmet
Off from his head ; on the ground he laid it,
    resplendently gleaming.
When he had tossed in his arms his well-
    loved son, and caressed him,
Then unto Zeus and the other immortals he
    made his petition :
" Zeus, and ye other immortals, I pray you
    that even as I am
So this boy may become pre-eminent over
    the Trojans,
Mighty and fearless as I, and in Ilios rule
    by his prowess !
May it hereafter be said, ' He is better by
    far than his father : '

(It is a verse any man might write in
golden letters on the wall of the chamber
where lies his first-born son : but we cannot
break off here, though the following lines are
an unwelcome reminder that Hector, like
Achilles, is a " splendid savage " after all !)

When he returns from the fray with the
    blood-stained armour of heroes,
When he has smitten the foe, and gladdened
    the heart of his mother.''
  So did he speak ; and into the arms of
    his wife, the belovèd,
Laid he the boy, and she in her fragrant
    bosom received him,
Laughing with tears in her eyes. Her hus-
    band was moved as he saw her :
'' Dear one, be not for me so exceedingly
    troubled in spirit.
No one against Fate's will shall send me
    untimely to Hades.
None among mortal men his destiny ever
    evadeth, —
Neither the coward nor hero, when once his
    doom is appointed.

  (Such fatalism is perhaps especially common to the soldierly temper in every age.)

Pray you, go to your home, and there give
    heed to your duties,
Tasks of the loom and the spindle, and lay
    your commands on the servants,
So they may work your will. Let men take
    thought for the combat,
All — I most of them all — whoso are in
    Ilios native.''

So having spoken, illustrious Hector took up the helmet,
Horsehair-crested. The faithful wife had homeward departed,
Turning ever about, and fast were her tears down dropping.
Presently now to her palace she came, that so fairly was builded,
Home of Hector, destroyer of heroes: many a servant
Found she within, and among them all she aroused lamentation.
They in his home over Hector lamented, while yet he was living,
Since they believed he would come no more from battle returning,
Nor would escape from the hands and might of the valiant Achaians.

(Il. VI. 237–502.)

These three women, Hecabè, Helen, and Andromache, appear again in the closing scenes of the drama. Hecabè in particular is seen quite frequently in the later books; and yet, she does not appeal to us, as the type of motherhood in bereavement, by any means so powerfully as might be expected. In fact, the dignity even of her queenly position is sadly lessened in our eyes, perhaps in the eyes of the ancient Greeks, by her apparently contented acquiescence in the conditions of a polygamous household. Sometimes she seems little better than the head of an Oriental harem. For example, in the last book, Priam, endeavouring to move Achilles' heart to pity, speaks as follows, with no touch of shame, feeling only the pathos of his own loss : —

> " Fifty numbered my sons when to Ilios
>   came the Achaians :
> Nineteen borne of a single mother to me,
>   and the others
> Children of women that dwelt in my royal
>   abode ; but already
> Now are the knees of the most by Ares the
>   furious broken."
>
> (Il. XXIV. 495–498.)

Such a half-brother, Gorgythion, falls at Hector's side in one of the earlier combats of the poem, and his mother, Castianeira, is there spoken of as " wedded," by Priam, " from Thrace, and like the goddesses in beauty."

Yet worse remains : when Hector tarries

alone outside the town to face the enraged
Achilles, Priam and Hecabè lean from the
wall together, bidding him have pity on
their gray hairs and come within the gates ;
and Priam says : —

"Nay, even now two sons, Polydoros and
        also Lycaon,
I am unable to see as the host throngs into
        the city.
These Laothoë bore unto me, — most noble
        of women.
If they still are alive in the Argive encamp-
        ment, surely
They shall be ransomed with gold and with
        bronze, for within is abundance.
Large was the dower illustrious Altes gave
        with his daughter.
If they already are dead and abide in the
        dwelling of Hades,
Bitter the sorrow will be to my heart and
        the mother who bore them."

(Il. XXII. 46-53.)

It is hard to believe that the poet who
created Andromache, — if this be indeed
his voice, — is unconscious how much he is
weakening Hecabè's hold upon our sympathies. There is, nevertheless, real pathos in

her words, which presently follow, though
they are but a brief pendant to a much
longer appeal of Priam.

> Tearing open her robe and revealing her
>   breast with the one hand,
> So she a tear let fall, and in wingèd words
>   she addrest him :
> "Hector, my child, this bosom revere, and
>   have pity upon me !
> If with my breast I ever have made thee
>   forgetful of sorrows,
> Now be mindful thereof, dear child, and,
>   avoiding the foeman,
> Enter within our walls ; stand not thus for-
>   ward to meet him.
> Merciless is he, and, if he shall slay thee,
>   never, my darling,
> I and thy bounteous wife on thy bed shall
>   lay thee, lamenting :
> Yon by the Argive vessels the swift-footed
>   dogs will devour thee."
>   (*Ibid.* 80–89.)

When her worst forebodings have been
realized, and Achilles drags Hector's life-
less body behind his chariot as he drives
exultantly shoreward, the pitiful group " in
the chamber over the gate " is again brought

distinctly into view, as it were to complete
the picture.

> And the mother
> Tore her hair, and flung far from her the
> beautiful head-dress,
> When she beheld her son, and loud and
> shrill she lamented.
> Pitiful, too, was the father's wail, and about
> him the people,
> Everywhere in the city, to moaning and
> weeping betook them.
> (Il. XXII. 405–409.)

But here again the father is unmistakably
made the chief figure. He can hardly be
restrained in his frenzy from rushing forth
at the gates to share his son's doom. He
fully realizes now that Hector was most
dear to him among all his children. Though
so many of his sons have fallen at Achilles'
hands, he mourns for Hector more than for
all the rest. He wishes he might at any
rate have held him dying in his arms : —

> "So we at least had sated ourselves with
> weeping and wailing,
> I myself, and the evil-fated mother who
> bore him."

So did he make his moan, and the towns-
 men groaning responded.
Then the Trojan women lamented, and
 Hecabè led them :
" Wretched am I, my child ! Why am I
 alive in my sorrow ?
Low thou liest in death, who by night and
 by day in our city
Ever my pride hast been, and to all our
 people a blessing,
Both to the men and the women of Troy.
 By all thou wert greeted
Like to a god : and indeed thou wert their
 honour and glory
During thy life ! Yet now thy death and
 doom are accomplished.''
(Ibid. 427–436.)

It illustrates excellently the wise mod-
eration and simplicity of the greatest artists, that Andromache is not present as
a witness of Hector's unworthy flight and
death. At this point we have again a
glimpse of her home-life, which is clearly
intended to recall that memorable earlier
scene in which she appeared.

   But Andromache knew not
Yet of her Hector's fate. No messenger
 came with the tidings,

Saying her husband had tarried outside of
 the gate of the city.
She was weaving a web, in the inmost room
 of her palace,
Twofold, purple, and many a flower she
 broidered upon it.

The quiet contrast with Helen's broidery
(*infra*, p. 44) is no accident, or at least one
of the divine accidents that befall only consummate genius.

Unto the serving-maids in her hall she had
 given commandment
Over the fire to set a mighty tripod, that
 Hector
Might have water, to bathe, when home-
 ward he came from the battle.
Hapless one! for she knew not that he, far,
 far from the bathing,
Under Achilles' hands by keen-eyed Pallas
 was vanquished.
Then from the tower she heard the shrieks
 and the voice of lamenting.
Trembling seized on her body, the shuttle
 was dropt from her fingers.
Straightway unto her fair-tressed serving-
 maids she commanded:
"Come ye twain with me to behold what
 deeds are accomplished.

That was the voice of my husband's rever-
    end mother.   Within me
Up to the lips my heart doth leap, and my
    knees are enfeebled ;
Surely calamity now draws nigh to the chil-
    dren of Priam.
Would that the tidings never might come
    to my ears !   But I fear me
Terribly, lest bold Hector alone by the god-
    like Achilles
Be cut off from the city, and unto the plain
    may be driven.
So ere now hath he ended the perilous pride
    that possessed him,
Since he never would stay in the midst of
    the ranks of his people.
Far to the vanward he hastened, in hardi-
    hood yielding to no man.''
Such were her words, and out of the hall as
    if frantic she darted.
Wildly her heart was throbbing ; and with
    her followed the maidens.
When to the battlements she was come,
    and the throng of the people,
There on the rampart taking her stand she
    gazed, and beheld him
Dragged in front of the town, and the swift-
    hooved steeds of Achilles
Merciless drew him along to the hollowed
    ships of the Argives.

Over her eyes like a veil descended the
    darkness of Hades.
Backward she fell in a swoon, and her soul
    fled out of her body.
Far from her head she cast the shining
    adornment upon it,
— Frontlet, and net for the hair, and head-
    band skilfully plaited,
Even her veil, — 'twas a gift from Aphro-
    dite the golden,
On that day whereon bright-helmeted Hec-
    tor had led her
Out of Eëtion's hall, having furnished num-
    berless bride-gifts.
Round her gathered the sisters of Hector,
    and wives of his brothers.
They in their midst upheld her, who nigh
    unto death was distracted.
When she again drew breath, and her soul
    had returned to her body,
Heavily sobbing she cried, in the midst of
    the women of Troia,
" Hector ! ill-fated am I ! to the selfsame
    doom we were nurtured,
Both of us : you in Troy, in the royal pal-
    ace of Priam,
I in Thebè, under the deep-wooded mountain
    of Plakos,
There in Eëtion's hall, who reared me when
    I was little !

Wretched were father and child! I would
    I had ne'er been begotten!
— Now unto Hades' abode in the depths of
    the earth thou departest.
I am behind thee left, in my bitter bereave-
    ment, a widow
Here in our halls: and our boy is yet but
    an infant and helpless,
Child of ill-starred parents, of me and of
    thee: and in nowise
Thou, when dead, and he, shall be to each
    other a comfort."

                       (Il. 437–486.)

(A passage of about twenty lines has
been omitted at this point from Andromache's lament. It is a somewhat famous
picture of an orphan's lot. He is described
as thrust aside by his father's friends while
they sit at the feast, as beaten, starved,
and thirsty. Surely this could not be the
lot of Hector's son while Troy stood un-
conquered. When Astyanax is directly
mentioned, it is as one who had fed " only
on marrow and fat flesh of sheep " : a
strange diet for an infant in the nurse's
arms! Ancient and modern students are
generally agreed that the verses cannot be

Homeric.) The following lines form the close of the twenty-second book, the central event of which is Hector's death : —

"Now by the curving Achaian vessels afar
        from thy parents,
When thou the hounds hast sated, the
        writhing worms shall devour thee.
Naked thou art, and yet in our palace the
        garments are ready,
Delicate beautiful garments, the handiwork
        of the women.
All these I will destroy in devouring flame :
        though in nowise
This will be helpful to thee, nor shalt thou
        within them be lying,
Yet among Trojan women and men it will
        bring to thee honour."
— Thus she lamenting spoke, and wailing
        responded the women.

(Il. 507–515.)

Only the two closing books of the great epic remain to be mentioned. The twenty-third is chiefly occupied with the games celebrated in Patroclos' honour. These scenes, naturally, afford little material suited to our present purpose. There is, however, a sinister reminder of the abundance of captive women, doubtless largely of gentle birth, held as prisoners in the camp. For the contest in wrestling, the first prize is a great tripod, intended for use over the fire, and estimated by the Greeks as of twelve oxen's worth. The " consolation " prize for the loser is a woman. Though " skilled in many tasks," she is valued only at four oxen. The victor in the chariot-race is to win both a woman and a tripod.

The poet, or poets, realized fully the effective contrast between these three un-happy matrons, — Andromache, Hecabè, Helen, — and the scenes of savage strife about them. We shall see them appear yet more prominently at the very close of the stately epic pageant. But yet, in regard to this trio, as well as the less prominent women of the Iliad, it should be kept always in mind that they are not intended to become, even for the time being, the chief object of interest. Each of them might indeed be so treated — and in fact every one of the three was so treated — in Euripidean tragedy. But here they are, so

G

to speak, not sculptured in the round, and refuse to be viewed as complete character-studies. Though drawn in firm and strong outlines, by a master's hand, they bear to the great temple of epic song merely the relation of figures in the frieze, or of the group upon a metope. One object of such a special study as the present paper is, to induce the reader to observe these same figures more carefully in their proper connection and environment, as component parts of the whole poem.

The Greeks reserved their highest admiration for devoted friendship or passionate love between men. Hence the bond of Achilles and Patroclos held the loftiest place in the appreciation of the classic people. The wedded happiness of Hector and Andromache appeals, it may be, more powerfully to us than to Homer's first hearers, certainly far more strongly than it did to Athenians of the fifth or fourth century B.C. Doubtless it was partly this feeling that led to the inclusion of Hector, not Achilles, among the three pagan knights, who, with three Jewish heroes and three

Christian champions, were held up for admiration in mediæval times as ideals of chivalry. Andromache is not, however, dwarfed or overshadowed even by her heroic and patriotic lord.

Of Helen this is not the place to speak at length. She can hardly be treated at all without the inclusion of the scene where she reappears, in the Odyssey, radiant, fascinating, and happy, despite all these years of shame, the well-loved wife of a contented Menelaos! Indeed, her figure is so frequently seen in later literature, of ancient and modern times, that it would not be easy to stop short of Goethe's Helena. As for Andrew Lang's collaboration in an audacious continuation of the Homeric story, in the form of a sensational prose romance, he himself realized the impiety of the attempt before it was fairly completed. We can only say Amen to his confession, — and accept his later volume, in defence of Homer's unity, as a manful palinode.

We have already indicated our feeling, that the epic treatment has weakened,

doubtless intentionally weakened, our natural sympathy with the sorrows of Hecabè.
The poet probably always remembers that
he is himself a Greek. Certainly he always
keeps it before us, that not only Paris, but
Troy, is utterly in the wrong. And it is
above all else the weak devotion and submission of the royal parents to Paris' lawless desire that draws down ruin upon all
Ilios as well as upon himself. It may be
that the polygamous life of the palace is to
be thought of as aiding in blinding their
eyes to the inexpiable nature of the wrong
done Menelaos.

These impressions are set down with
somewhat more confidence, because we
find, present in the poem, a purer, more
beautiful, and, upon the whole, a more
pathetic figure of motherhood in sorrow,
than that of Hecabè. It is a character
which at first thought may seem to lie
beyond the limits of our announced subject. I mean the sea-nymph Thetis, the
mother of Achilles.

Homer's divinities in general do not appear to be taken quite seriously even by

their creator. Closely interwoven as they are with the plot, they can rarely be said to control it. Indeed events would apparently take much the same course without them. Though we may not feel all the grim indignation of Plato as we watch their actions, we can hardly fail to agree with him, that they are surprisingly bad models of behaviour to set before the youthful mind. The childish temper of the goddesses, in particular, culminates in the astonishing scene of the twenty-first book, where nearly all the divinities take part, in almost ludicrous fashion, with Greeks or Trojans in the fray. Hera, irritated by a bold word from Artemis' lips, has seized both the maiden's wrists in her left hand, and with the right

> Smiling
> Beat her over the ears, while this way and
> that she was turning.
>
> (Il. XXI. 491-492.)

The weapon used in this chastisement is the huntress' own bow and quiver, and the arrows fall meanwhile far and wide in the dust. Presently, when released, the archer-maid flies for comfort to her august father, who, smiling, holds her upon his knee while she bitterly complains of his ill-tempered spouse, — mother Leto meantime carefully gathering up the scattered arrows. Of this remarkable family we are content to see little more, as the epic gathers yet greater dignity and force through the closing books.

But Thetis is hardly of their kin, in no sense of their kind; and though she is a divinity, dwelling with the rest of her race in the depths of the sea, it is in a wholly human relation and character that she so often meets us in the Iliad.

As to the unique and undying charm of the silvery-footed Nereid, we appeal fearlessly to every schoolboy. (That is, to Macaulay's schoolboy, whom we may fitly set here to face the New Zealander invoked in our prologue.) Any one who has read the tale, no matter how painfully scanned through the darkened window of a Greek text, cannot have forgotten the thrill of pleasure, the full assurance that we were indeed in the land of Enchantment, that came over us at the point where Achilles' tearful appeal upon the lonely strand is instantly answered : —

And his reverend mother did hear him
Where in the depths of the sea by her
   ancient sire she was sitting.
                    (Il. I. 357–358.)
Though

Like a mist from the brine she uprises,
                    (*Ibid.* 359.)

yet the goddess is at once lost in the mother as she takes her place beside her mortal son. And under her caressing hand the strong-souled warrior is again but a weeping boy at that mother's knee. He gladly obeys her bidding to repeat to her all the story of his wrongs, though well aware that she is already as familiar with it as himself. In his appeal for her intercession, we catch a glimpse of that marvellous childhood in the royal halls of Thessaly, and yet beyond we hear also the murmur of strange discord in the divine world, which could hardly have come, save through her lips, even to the ears of the inspired bard.

For Achilles recalls to his mother how in childhood he had heard her tell that she alone had once saved the tottering throne of Zeus, when brother, wife, and favourite daughter conspired against him and would have compassed his downfall. Yet even this reminder of her wondrous power is offered only as a reason why she may well intercede at Zeus' knees for justice to her child. The tears of mother and son are for a moment commingled, and she bitterly bewails the day when she bore him to brief life and a grievous doom. It was in truth utterly against her own will, doubtless through actual guile and force combined, that this free daughter of the billowy sea had submitted to a mortal husband. Yet once wedded, and a mother, she tarried with seeming content in the abode of the human father of her Achilles.

It may be well to assure a modern reader of Homer that Thetis is no mere elemental spirit, like the Undines of our northern world of myth, who acquire a soul and hope of immortality from this union with man. The divinities of the Greeks are like mankind ; in fact, early poets assure us that they were sprung from the same source. But the differences are wholly in the favour of the divine natures, who lack nothing which man has to bestow.

It was doubtless only the bond of maternal love that detained Thetis in Peleus' home, for, now that Achilles is in the Troad, she also has returned to Nereus' submarine palace in this quarter of the Ægean, to be ever close at hand in her son's time of need.

At the earliest possible moment, Thetis does betake herself to snowy Olympos, and obtains from Zeus the promise of just vengeance upon Agamemnon. Here the temptation lies especially near, to interpret her as the mere embodied type of divine mother-love itself, traversing sea, earth, and heaven in her devotion, and interceding at the very Throne of Grace for suffering, wronged humanity. But such a fancy is no doubt foreign to the intention of the poet, for whom Thetis is as real a person as any actor in the tale.

Wherever she reappears, it is because

the same chord of maternal affection is struck. Everywhere we see the silvery flash of her tireless feet, the tender grace of divine motherhood, the sad prescience of mourning soon to be. The most learned critic of antiquity erased three lines from his edition of the poem, because they laid upon her lips a sentiment unworthy of the mother.

Her most important later appearance is when she comes to console Achilles for Patroclos' death, and thence departs to Hephaistos' abode on Olympos, in quest of fresh armour to replace that stripped by Hector from Patroclos slain. It is with a heavy heart that she thus proceeds to equip her hero for his last and greatest exploit, for she has just reminded Achilles:—

Shortlived truly, my child, thou'lt be, from the words thou hast uttered,
Since at once after Hector for thee too death is appointed.

(Il. XVIII. 95, 96.)

The culminating scene of Thetis' life as a mother does not come within the limits of our subject, for Achilles is yet alive when the poem closes. This very fact, however, may serve to emphasize what has been said elsewhere, that the pathetic characters of the Iliad exist not for their own sake, but purely to serve the requirements of the epic plot. From a special study like the present essay it is peculiarly desirable to return to a thoughtful perusal of the poem *as a whole.* And the last phrase is chosen advisedly. There is no more imperative duty for the teacher of literature, than to encourage the study of the Iliad and the Odyssey, and indeed of all other great poems, as wholes: as the masterpieces of ideal artists, appealing, like a Madonna Sistina or a heaven-piercing Gothic spire, to the noblest of human faculties, — the imagination.

III

CLOSING SCENES OF THE ILIAD

HECTOR is killed at the end of the fourth day of actual fighting, the twenty-seventh since the action of the epic began. Neither side resumes the struggle, within the limits of the Iliad. The following day is spent by the Greeks in cremating Patroclos' body, together with captive Trojans, animals, and various treasures. Still another day is devoted to the erection of a huge barrow over the pyre, and to funeral games celebrated about it, in honour of Achilles' gentle friend. At this point the twenty-third book closes, and the final rhapsody begins.

The author of Iliad XXIV., whether we call him Homer or not, was certainly a masterful artist, who composed this book for the important place it now occupies, at the close of the great epic. No other part of the work has so deep a pathos, so noble an ethical tone, or a more elaborate structure. No portion will better repay a thoughtful study of detail. The book is, however, more than eight hundred lines in length. Within our limits we can at best only note the chief features, in a rapid outline.

It is easy to illustrate from almost any scene, in this most ancient of European epics, how entirely every great poet must rely for his strongest effects upon motives which are essentially human and universal. We may repeat, of Priam's lament for his sons, what Longfellow sings of David in his bereavement : —

> "There is no far nor near,
>   There is neither there nor here,
>   There is neither soon nor late,
>   In that Chamber over the Gate,
>   Nor any long ago
>   To that cry of human woe,
>   O Absalom, my son !"

The book begins with an allusion to the athletic contests by Patroclos' mound, which are just completed. This passage may be regarded as a sort of dramatic prologue, outlining the situation at which the action begins.

> The games were done. The folk to
>   their swift ships
> Dispersing went. Of supper and sweet
>   sleep
> They thought, to be enjoyed. Achilles
>   wept,
> Remembering his dear comrade. Nor did
>   sleep,
> The all-conquering, hold him. To and fro
>   he tossed,
> Missing Patroclos' bloom and glorious might.
> What toils he had wrought with him, and
>   woes endured,
> Cleaving the wars of men, and grievous
>   waves, —
> These he recalled, and dropped a swelling
>   tear.
> Sometimes upon his side, then on his back,
> He lay, or face ; again he rose erect,
> And madly whirled along the beach. The
>   Dawn
> Escaped him not, that shone on sea and
>   shore.
> When he had yoked his swift steeds to the
>   car,

Hector he bound to drag behind the team,
And drew him thrice round dead Patroclos'
    mound,
Then rested in his hut; but left the foe
Prone in the dust outstretched. Yet from
    his form
Apollo kept all harm, pitying the man,
Though dead, and screened him wholly with
    his shield
Of gold, lest he who dragged should tear
    his flesh.

(Il. XXIV. 1–21.)

. We must endeavour to have a clear picture
of the scene. The Trojans, shut within the
beleaguered walls, look forward, from day
to day, in hopeless suspense, to the doom
which Hector's fall has made inevitable.
The Greeks, equally inactive, await in their
camp the hour when Achilles shall put off
his grief and lead them to victory. And
Achilles himself, like a lioness bereft of
her young, lies brooding in the empty lair,
insults from day to day the unconscious
body of his enemy, — and forgets the call
of valour. After this outrage had been
repeated for twelve successive days, the
gods become angry, and debate if they

shall send down the divine messenger,
Hermes, to steal the body away. Instead
of this, Iris is finally despatched to summon
Achilles' mother, the sea-nymph Thetis, to
the heavenly council. The gentle goddess
of the rainbow instantly darts earthward,
and plunges into the dark waters of the
Ægean, beneath which is the abode of
Thetis' father, Nereus, the old man of the
sea. The poet continues : —

And Thetis in the hollow cave she found,
Where all the other sea divinities
Were gathered round her ; and among them
    she
Bewailed the fate of her illustrious son,
Whose doom it was in fertile Troy to die,
Far from the fatherland. Then, standing
    near,
Iris of nimble feet addressed her thus :
" Thetis, arise ; for Zeus, whose councils are
Immortal, summons thee."
                 The goddess then,
The silver-footed Thetis, answered her : —
" Why hath that mighty god commanded
    me ?
I shrink from mingling with the immortals,
    since

Unnumbered sorrows in my heart have I,
Yet will I go.   Not vain the word shall be
Which he may utter."   When she had spoken
        thus,
The mighty goddess took a dusky robe,
Than which no darker raiment she might
        find,
And went.   The swift, wind-footed Iris led,
And the sea's wave was round about them
        cleft.   (*Ibid.* 83–96.)

The black robe is of course, as with us,
the emblem of mourning; in this case as
much for Achilles as for Patroclos.   It is,
in fact, one of the frequent reminders of the
tragic scenes which lie in part beyond the
limits of the poem itself.

Reaching the shore they darted to the sky,
And found wide-seeing Zeus; and all the rest,
Blessèd immortal gods, assembled sate.
Then Thetis took her seat by father Zeus,
— Pallas made way for her, — and Hera put
A lovely golden cup into her hand,
Comforting her with words.   Then Thetis
        drank,
And gave the cup again; and unto them
The sire of gods and men began to speak.
                              (*Ibid.* 97–103.)

H

This passage tempts us aside to a somewhat elaborate comparison. This book is
beyond question the artistic culmination of
the epic. So the Panathenaic frieze is the
chief glory of the Parthenon, and unrivalled
among extant reliefs, at least. This opening scene in the Olympian council-hall, then,
may, not unnaturally, be set beside the
figures of the twelve great gods upon the
temple's eastern front. Now, if in the
frieze the central group about the priest
— which should doubtless be regarded as
ideally upon a different level — be elimi-
nated, Zeus and Hera from the one side,
Pallas Athene from the other, are brought
close together. A corner of the Zeus-block
was long missing. The complete excavations of recent years upon the Acropolis
brought to light few things more interesting
than the little triangular fragment. In the
wingèd figure upon it, Dr. Charles Waldstein
at once recognized Iris ; so no figure of our
Homeric group is now missing from the
relief, except, of course, the rare guest,
Thetis. Zeus' bidding is that Thetis go
straightway to her son, and inform him of

the gods' command.   He must accept a ransom, and give up Hector's body.   Thetis
immediately

Went darting from Olympos' summit down

to carry this message.   To Achilles she
says, after a few consolatory words : —

" Hearken at once to me.   A messenger
Of Zeus to thee am I.   He says the gods
Are wroth, and he himself enraged at thee
Beyond the immortals all, since with mad
          heart
Thou keepest Hector by the curving ships,
And hast not given him back.   But do thou
          now
Release him.   Take the ransom for the
          dead."
Achilles, fleet of foot, thus answered her :
" So be it.   Whoso brings the ransom, he
May take the body, since with earnest mind
The Olympian hath himself commanded it."
                          (*Ibid.* 133–140.)

Meanwhile, Iris is again sent down by Zeus,
this time to the venerable King Priam, who
is bidden to go to Achilles under cover of
the night, carrying precious gifts, and ac-

companied only by one aged herald.   He is
assured of a safe return under the protec-
tion of Hermes.

It was remarked by the ancients that Iris
was regularly employed as messenger in the
Iliad, Hermes in the Odyssey.   The appearance of the god in the last episode of the
poem is, therefore, sometimes counted as
one of many indications pointing to a somewhat later origin.   But in truth both Iris
and Hermes, as well as Thetis, are here busy
as couriers, and, indeed, all the divine forces
are exerted to bring about the culminating
scene of the great drama.   Omitting the
speech of Iris to Priam, we continue : —

Fleet-footed Iris, speaking thus, was gone.
But he descended to his vaulted room,
High-roofed, of cedar, that much treasure
    held.
Hecabè, too, his wife, he called, and said :
" Dame, an Olympian messenger is come
To me, and bade me ransom my dear son,
Seeking the Achaians' ships, and thither
    bring
Gifts for Achilles which shall melt his heart.
Come, tell me how it seems unto thy mind ;
For mightily my own desire and heart

Are urging me to go to yonder ships,
Within the Achaians' wide-extended camp."
  So Priam spoke.   His wife bemoaned, and
        said :
" Ah me !   Where now is fled thy sense, for
        which
Thou wert renowned to strangers, and among
The folk thou rulest !   How canst thou desire
To fare alone unto the Achaians' ships,
Before the face of him who has despoiled
Thy many valiant sons ?   Thy heart is hard
As iron !   For if he have thee in his power,
And see thee with his eyes, that savage man
And faithless, he will have no reverence
Nor pity for thee.   Nay, let us now sit
Here in our halls afar, and mourn.   For him
Even thus the mighty Fate did spin her
        thread,
When he was born of me, that he should sate
The hounds fleet-footed, far away from us
His parents, in that forceful hero's power
Whose heart's core I could seize on and
        devour !
Thus for my son a deed of recompense
Were wrought !   He slew him, who had
        wronged him not,
But only stood forth to defend the men
Of Troy and the deep-bosomed Trojan dames,
Nor ever thought of terror and of flight."
                              (*Ibid.* 188–216.)

This last line is a curious and interesting
one.   Hecabè (or can it be even her poet?)
knows nothing of that dishonourable flight
of Hector thrice about the circle of the city's
wall, against which Andrew Lang protests,
as a calumny of Homer, in his beautiful
poem, Helen of Troy.

Then agèd, godlike Priam answered her:
" Do not detain me when I long to go,
And do not be for me in our own halls
An evil omen.   Thou wilt not dissuade me.
If any other one of men on earth,
Of seers who watch the offerings, or of priests,
Had bidden me, we would have accounted it
A lie, and rather would have held aloof.
But now — for I heard the god myself, and
        gazed
Into her face — I go, nor vain shall be
The word.   But if it be my destiny
By the bronze-mailed Achaians' ships to die,
I am willing.   Let Achilles slay me at once,
Clasping within these arms my son, when I
Have sated my desire for grief."

                        He spoke,
And from the chests took off the shapely lids.
Then he chose forth twelve very lovely
        shawls,

Twelve single cloaks thereto, as many rugs,
So many robes, and just as many doublets;
Two tripods brightly gleaming, and four
    caldrons;
A very lovely cup besides, which men
Of Thrace had given him, when he had come
    upon
An embassy, — a precious thing: nor yet
Did the old man grudge from his halls e'en
    this,
But in his heart exceedingly desired
To ransom his dear son.
                (*Ibid.* 217–237.)

Priam, who seems half crazed with grief
and excitement, bursts forth into bitter
reproaches against the Trojans who are
gathered under the gateway of his house,
and, calling angrily by name upon nine of
his surviving sons, bids them harness mules
to the wagon which shall bear these treasures toward the hostile camp on the shore.
This they do, and also attach Priam's horses
to his own chariot. This has all occurred
in the courtyard within the royal palace.

But Hecabè with troubled soul drew nigh,
Holding the wine, like honey to the heart,

In her right hand, within a golden bowl,
That they might pour libation ere they went.
(*Ibid.* 283–285.)

It will be remembered that Hecabè appears in a very similar manner, with wine in her hand, when she comes to meet Hector in the sixth book. This repetition of the same *motif* has sometimes been regarded as a clear case of imitation, betraying a new and younger hand.

Standing before the steeds, she spoke, and
    said :
" So do thou pour to father Zeus, and pray
That thou shalt from the foemen home re-
    turn,
Since thine own spirit urges thee indeed
Unto the ships, — though I desire it not !
But do thou pray to cloud-wrapped Kronos'
    son,
Dwelling on Ida, who looks down on all
The Trojan land, and ask an ominous bird,
His speedy messenger, which is most dear
Of birds to him, and mightiest in strength,
Appearing on the right : so thou thyself,
Seeing it with thine eyes, trustful therein
Mayst fare unto the fleet-horsed Danaäns'
    ships.

But if wide-seeing Zeus give not to thee
His messenger, I would not urge thee on,
Nor to the Argives' vessels bid thee go,
Exceedingly impetuous as thou art.''
And answering her, the godlike Priam said:
''O wife, I will not disobey thee when
Thou urgest me to this; for it is well
To lift our hands to Zeus, if he perchance
Will pity us.'' Thus the old man spoke,
    and bade
A housemaid pour clear water on his hands.
She stood beside him, holding in her hands
A bowl and pitcher; then when he had
    cleansed
His hands, he from his wife received the cup.
Then taking in the courtyard's midst his
    stand

(here was the great altar of Zeus, and on
this very spot, not many days later, the
venerable king was to meet his death,
before the eyes of his wife and daughters,
on the night when Troy was taken),

He prayed, and poured the wine, looking
    meanwhile
Into the sky, and thus he spoke aloud:
''O father Zeus, from Ida holding sway,
Most glorious and most mighty, do thou
    grant

That I unto Achilles' dwelling come
Welcomed and pitied ; and send thou a bird
Of omen, thy swift messenger, which is
Most dear of birds to thee, and mightiest
In strength, upon the right, that I myself,
Beholding him, may go, trustful therein,
Unto the vessels of the swift-horsed Greeks."
(Ibid. 286–313.)

A black eagle instantly appears in the
sky, on the right, flying over the city.
Then the two old men start forth confi-
dently and in eager haste ; the herald driv-
ing the mule-team, and Priam following
upon his chariot. The royal kinsfolk and
other Trojans escort them, lamenting, but
turn back at the gates.

But not unmarked by far-beholding Zeus
They on the plain appeared. And when he
    saw
The agèd man, he pitied him. At once
To Hermes, his belovèd son, he spoke :
" O Hermes, since to thee it is most dear
To be man's comrade, and thou hearkenest
To whom thou wilt. hie thee and go ; conduct
Priam unto the Achaians' hollow ships,
So that no other of the Danai
Shall see or notice him, until he comes

To Peleus' son." He spoke. The Argus-
    slayer,
The messenger, obeyed : and straightway
    then
Under his feet the lovely sandals bound,
Ambrosial, golden, which upon the sea
Bear him, and over boundless earth, as swift
As gusts of wind. He took his wand, where-
    with
The eyes of men he entrances, whom he will,
And rouses others from their sleep again :
With this in hand flew the stout Argus-
    slayer.
Troy and the Hellespont he quickly reached.
(Ibid. 331–346.)

Under the guise of a goodly mortal youth,
Hermes presents himself to the two fright-
ened old men, just at dusk, when they have
reached the river, on their way to the shore,
and offers to guide them. He pretends to
be an esquire of Achilles. He assures Priam
that Hector's body lies uncorrupted and
unsoiled, and that his many wounds have
miraculously closed. Priam, to secure the
youth's faithful guidance, offers him the
precious cup which was intended for Achilles. But the god replies : —

" Old sir, thou'rt tempting me, a younger
        man,
But wilt not win me,—thou who biddest me,
Without Achilles' knowledge, take thy gift.
I stand in fear of him, and dread in heart
To rob him, lest hereafter woe befall
To me.   But as thy escort I would go
E'en to famed Argos, fitly guiding thee,
By land, or vessel swift.   No one, forsooth,
Disdainful of thy guide, would strive with
        thee."   (*Ibid.* 433–439.)

The god seems to give us a glimpse of his
divine nature, as he proudly assures the
timid king that under his guidance he might
pass unmolested, not merely to the hostile
camp on the shore, but even far into the
native land of his foes.   A god is rarely
able to conceal his divinity altogether.

Thus speaking, Hermes on the chariot
        leaped,
And quickly grasped the scourge and reins
        in hand.
Into the horses and the mules he breathed
Glorious force.   But when they now were
        come
To the intrenchments of the ships, and moat,
The guards were just employed about their
        meal.

Upon them all the herald, the Argus-slayer,
Poured sleep, and pushed the bar, and, opening
The gates, led in the old man, and splendid gifts
Upon the car.   (*Ibid.* 440–447.)

The divine intervention is, it will be noticed, essential to Priam's success. Such passages as this are very different from those where Pallas appears to Achilles, or Aphrodite to Helen, remaining invisible to all others. In those scenes the divinities are perhaps little more than poetic figures for the voice of wisdom or of passion in the human heart itself. Here, on the contrary, Hermes is as real to the poet, and to his hearers, as the old king himself.

But now when they were come
Unto Pelides' lofty cabin, which
The Myrmidons had builded for their lord :
Hewing the beams of fir ; and overhead
They thatched it, mowing in the meadow land
The downy rush ; and round about they made
A spacious courtyard for their lord, with stakes

Close set.   The gate a single bar held fast,
Of pine, which three Achaians pushed in
    place,
And three would open the great bolted
    gate,
Of other men : Achilles even alone
Would push it home.

(Ibid. 448–456.)

The poet has forgotten Priam, for the moment, over his description of Achilles' abode. (Such comparisons as this between the physical strength of the chieftains and of common men are very frequent in Homer. The reader will remember, for instance, how Hector, assaulting the Greek lines, poises and casts with ease a stone which, as the poet says,

Three men could hardly heave into a wain,
Such as are now alive.

The most curious example, however, is the venerable Nestor and his mighty punch-bowl :

Scarce could another from the table raise
The bowl, when full ; but Nestor, although
    old,
Easily lifted it.

Another passage for Horace — and for
Holmes !)

    Hermes, the Helper, then, for the old man
Opened the gate, and led the splendid gifts
For fleet Achilles in ; then to the earth
Descended from the chariot, and said :
" O agèd man, I, an undying god,
Hermes, am come. My father bade me be
Thy guide. But now will I depart again,
Nor meet Achilles' eyes. 'Twere cause for
          wrath
If an immortal god so openly
Should show his friendliness for human
          kind.
But go thou in, and clasp Achilles' knees."
Thus speaking, Hermes was already gone
To broad Olympos. From his chariot
Priam leaped down to earth ; and there he
          left
Idaios, who remained to hold the mules
And steeds. Straight toward the house the
          old man went,
Where, dear to Zeus, Achilles had his home.
He found him there within. Apart from
          him
His comrades had their places. Only two,
Heroic Automedon, and Alkimos
Of Ares' stock, were busy in his presence.

Achilles was just ceasing from his meal,
From drink and food.   The table stood by
    him.
Great Priam entered in unmarked by them,
And close beside Achilles took his place,
Clasped with both hands his knees, and
    kissed
Those awful murderous hands, which had
    destroyed
His many sons.
                  As when a mighty curse
Befalleth one who in his fatherland
Hath slain a man, and to another folk
He comes, unto some wealthy man's abode,
And wonder seizes those who look on him,
So did Achilles marvel, as he saw
The godlike Priam ; and the others too
In their amazement gazed at one another.
Then Priam prayerfully addressed him thus :
" Remember, O Achilles, like the gods,
Thy father, even of such years as I,
Upon the fatal threshold of old age.
Perchance the neighbours vex him round
    about,
And there is no one to avert from him
Calamity and ruin.   But yet he,
Hearing thou art alive, exults in heart,
And all his days is hopeful he shall see
His well-loved son returning home from
    Troy.

But wholly evil is my fate, who had
The noblest sons in wide Troy-land, and
    none
Of them, I tell thee, now is left alive.
Fifty I had when the Achaians came:
Nineteen were from one womb born unto
    me,
The others of the women in my halls.
Of most, impetuous Ares brake the knees.''

(Here, as often, Ares is a mere vague per-
sonification of war.)

"Him who alone remained, and kept my
    town
And people, thou the other day hast slain.
While he was fighting for his fatherland:
Hector.   For his sake to the Achaians'
    ships
I came, to buy him back from thee, and
    bring
A priceless ransom.   But do thou revere
The gods, Achilles, and have pity on me,
Remembering thine own father.   Yet am I
More piteous, and have borne what no one
    else
Of men on earth has done,—to lift the hand
Of him who slew my son unto my lips.''
   So spoke he; and he roused indeed in him
Desire of weeping for his father.   Then

I

Grasping him by the hand, he gently pushed
The old man from him; and they both be-
    wailed
Unceasingly: the one remembering
Hector, the slayer of men, the while he lay
Before Achilles' feet; but for his sire
Achilles wept, and for Patroclos too
At times; and in the house their moan went
    up.
But when divine Achilles had his fill
Of wailing, straightway from his chair he
    rose,
And lifted by the hand the agèd man,
Pitying his hoary head and hoary beard.
Addressing him, he uttered wingèd words:
"Ah, wretched one, thou hast indeed endured
Full many woes in heart. How didst thou
    dare
To come to the Achaians' ships, alone,
Into my presence, — mine, who have de-
    spoiled
Thy many noble sons? Thy soul is hard
As iron. But, come sit upon a chair,
And we will truly let our sorrows lie
Quiet within our hearts, grieved though we
    be;
For in chill mourning there is no avail,
Since so the gods have spun for wretched
    men,
To live in sorrow. They are free from care!

For at the door of Zeus two jars are set,
One filled with evil gifts, and one again
With blessings ; and to whomsoever Zeus,
Hurler of lightning, intermingling gives,
He chances now on evil, now on good ;
But him to whom he gives but ills he makes
A byword !   Wretched famine urges him
Over the holy earth.   He wanders forth,
Unhonoured of the gods or mortal men.''
(Ibid. 457–533.)

No man, it seems, has unmixed happiness : but some have none !

It was for such passages as this that Plato was unwilling to admit Homer into his republic.   It would perhaps hardly be just to ascribe these sentiments to the poet himself.   All Achilles' joy in life, all his faith in the fairness or the kindness of the gods, perished with Patroclos.   It has been, however, very truly remarked (by Professor Thomas Davidson) that in the closing books of the Iliad, as a whole, we find little trace of that delight in life which we are wont to regard as a peculiarly Greek feeling.

" So the gods gave to Peleus glorious gifts
At birth,—for he to all mankind was famed

For bliss and wealth, and ruled the Myr-
    midons.
A goddess, too, they made his wife, though
    he
Was mortal. Yet the god sent woe on him;
For in his halls no race of mighty sons
Arose ; one all-untimely child had he,
And I protect him not as he grows old :
Since far from home, I tarry in the Troad,
Vexing thee and thy children. And of thee
'Tis said, old sir, that thou wert happy
    once.
Of all the land which Lesbos, Makar's home,
Doth bound, and Phrygia, and vast Helles-
    pont,
Of all these folk, 'tis said, thou wert supreme,
O agèd man, in wealth and tale of sons.
But since the heaven-dwellers on thee sent
This sorrow, ever round thy town is strife
And slaying of men.
          Endure, and do not grieve
Unceasingly in spirit. Naught by grief
Wilt thou accomplish for thy gallant son ;
Thou mayst not raise him up to life again ;
Nay, sooner wilt thou suffer other ills."

(Ibid. 534–551.)

The last line is perhaps a warning that
Achilles feels rising within himself an un-

reasoning rage, in response to this wild passion of grief over his fallen enemy, Hector. If such is his meaning, Priam does not realize it.

Then agèd, godlike Priam answered him:
"Bid me not yet to sit upon a chair,
Thou child of Zeus, while Hector in thy
    house
Uncared-for lies. But give him up at once,
That I may see him, and accept the price."
                  (*Ibid.* 552–555.)

But the fierce and haughty spirit of Achilles is aroused at this urgent appeal for immediate action. We must not allow ourselves to imagine that Homer's men are mediæval knights or Elizabethan gentlemen, by any means. There is much of the savage in them still. But Achilles, at any rate, realizes the danger, — and also the wickedness of any harm done to his suppliant guest.

Then swift Achilles with fierce glance
    replied :
"Chafe me no more, old sir ; I do myself
Intend to give thee Hector back. From
    Zeus

As messenger to me my mother came,
The daughter of the Ancient of the sea.
And as for thee, O Priam, well I know
In heart, and it escapes me not, some god
Guided thee to the Achaians' speedy ships;
For never mortal man would dare to come,
Though youthful, to our camp, nor could
    he elude
The guards, nor easily push back the bolts
Upon our gates.   So do thou rouse no more,
O agèd man, mine anger in my grief,
Lest I may leave thee not unharmed, even
    here
Within my cabin, suppliant as thou art,
But may transgress against the will of Zeus."
  He spoke; the agèd man in fear obeyed.
Pelides like a lion through the house
Rushed to the portal; not alone: with him
Two servants went, heroic Automedon
And Alkimos, whom of his comrades most
Achilles honoured, save Patroclos dead.
They from the yoke released the steeds and
    mules,
And led the herald of the old king in,
And bade him sit.   Then from the shining
    cart
They took the priceless ransom for the
    head
Of Hector. But two robes they left, and
    one

Tunic well-knit, that he might wrap there-
    with
The dead, and give him to be carried home.
Calling the maids, he ordered them to wash
And to anoint him, taking him apart,
That Priam might not look upon his son,
Lest in his sorrowing spirit he might not
Restrain his wrath when he beheld his child;
And so Achilles' heart would be aroused,
And he would slay him, and transgress the
    will
Of Zeus.   *(Ibid.* 559–586.)

When the body has been prepared for
the bier, Achilles himself aids in laying it
upon the chariot. Yet his reluctance and
misgivings find utterance meanwhile in a
prayer to his dead friend : —

        " Patroclos, be not wroth,
Even in Hades, that I have released
The mighty Hector for his loving father.
For no unworthy ransom did he give,
And with thee I will share it, as is right."
                  (Ibid. 592–595.)

It is interesting to remember that until
Patroclos appeared to his friend in a vision
after death Achilles had hardly believed in
any continued existence beyond the tomb.

Indeed, it is hard to resist the feeling that the hero was at times, even to the Homeric poets, as he certainly became to the later Greeks, an ideal type of the short-lived youth of man, clinging to life, shuddering at the very thought of death. Strikingly characteristic still is the apparition of his shade in Hades, described in the Odyssey among the adventures of Odysseus. Even there he resents fiercely the attempt to soften the wretchedness of life in the land of shades, and finds his only consolation in the thought that his son is a gallant warrior still, up there in the sunshine.

Achilles, returning into the cabin, takes his place, facing Priam, against the opposite wall; perhaps at a safe distance from his guest. He addresses the unhappy monarch : —

    " Thy son is freed, old man, as thou hast
        bid,
And lies upon the bier.   At dawn shalt thou
Behold and bear him hence.   But now let us
Take thought of supper.   Even Niobe
Of the fair hair took thought for food."
(Ibid. 599-602.)

The tale of the unfortunate daughter of Tantalus, which is here repeated by Achilles, need not be transcribed. More interesting for us is the allusion to a curious rock formation near Magnesia, in Asia Minor, which has been known for countless centuries as the weeping Niobe : —

"Now on the lonely mountains, mid the rocks
On Sipylos, where, so 'tis said, the nymphs
Have their abode, who dance about the stream
Of Acheloion, as a stone she stands,
Enduring sorrows sent her by the gods."
(Ibid. 614–617.)

We are informed that these lines were rejected by the greatest Homeric scholar among the ancients, the librarian Aristarchos, on the ground that they were irrelevant. This very fact, however, indicates that they are at least very ancient, if not originally a part of the scene. The figure thus alluded to is a sort of high-relief against a background of natural rock. The shape is thrice the human height, and some two hundred feet from the ground. A trickling spring is said to give the impression of falling tears. Whoever composed these lines was familiar with this locality of Asia Minor, and hence the passage has been drawn into the discussion over the origin of the Homeric poems. Perhaps it has aided, with other local allusions, to give to Smyrna a certain pre-eminence among Homer's many birthplaces.

Achilles now kills a sheep, the meal is prepared, and Priam silently partakes of bread and meat, doubtless less from hunger than from dread of rousing the wrath of his terrible host.

> When they had sated them with food and
>   drink,
> Dardanian Priam at Achilles gazed
> In wonder, seeing him so tall and fair.
> Achilles, too, admired Dardanian Priam,
> Viewing his goodly aspect, giving ear
> Unto his words.   But when they had looked
>   their fill
> At one another, first unto his host
> The venerable, godlike Priam spoke:
> " Let me at once, O child of Zeus, lie down,
> That we of slumber sweet may have our fill,
> And rest.   Not yet mine eyes beneath their
>   lids

Have closed, since at thy hands my son
    gave up
His life, but evermore I groan aloud,
And brood on my innumerable griefs,
Rolling in filth within my courtyard's close.
Now truly have I tasted food, and let
The gleaming wine pass down my throat.
    Before
I had tasted nothing."   (*Ibid.* 628–642.)

The great strain upon the old king's mind
is relieved, at least in part. Though he
has not yet seen Hector's body, he knows
that his mission is to be successfully accomplished. So exhausted Nature asserts herself. Doubtless, as has been said, he breaks
his fast more through fear to rouse Achilles'
anger than from hunger. But, having eaten
and drunk, the need of rest overcomes him,
even in the house of his son's slayer. There
is something strangely pathetic in this un-
complaining reference to his fortnight-long
fast and vigil, and in the overwhelming desire for sleep now, though he is still in the
lion's claws.

The beds are spread under the colonnade
in the courtyard. It must not be imagined

that this is scant courtesy to a guest, nor an
improbable device of the tale in order to
facilitate Priam's escape in the night.   In
the Odyssey, Telemachos and the son of
Nestor are lodged, together, in precisely the
same manner at Menelaos' home, and, indeed, in Nestor's own palace as well.   Achilles, moreover, explains that his guests are
thus more secure from being seen by any
Greeks less kindly-minded than himself.
Before they part for the night, however, a
most generous, we may indeed fairly say a
chivalric, thought occurs to Achilles, and he
asks his guest : —

" But prithee tell me, and say truthfully
How many days thou dost intend to pay
The rites to mighty Hector, so that I
Myself may wait, and hold my folk aloof."
Then agèd, godlike Priam answered him :
" If thou indeed dost wish me to complete
Great Hector's burial, by acting thus,
Achilles, thou wouldst win my gratitude.
Thou knowest we are pent within the town,
The wood is from the mountain far to fetch,
And much in fear the Trojans.   We would
      wail
Nine days for him within our halls, and on

The tenth would bury him, and the folk
    would feast.
The eleventh we could rear a mound for
    him,
And on the twelfth will fight, if needs must
    be."

(The last words with a despairing sigh, no
doubt.)

    The great Achilles, fleet of foot, replied:
" These things shall be for thee as thou dost
    bid,
And even for so long a time will I
Put off the war as thou commandest me."
(Ibid. 656–670.)

So the exhausted king and his old herald
lie down to rest under the portico; and
Achilles also sleeps, at Briseis' side, within
the cabin.

But in the night Hermes comes again,
warns Priam of his danger, and leads him
safely from the Greek encampment. At
the ford of the Scamander Hermes van-
ishes, and day dawns. As the two aged
men approach the town, they are descried
by Cassandra, and the wailing folk meet
the returning king at the gate, Hector's

wife and mother at their head, but Priam
presses on to his palace.

> When they had brought him to that
> famous home,
> They laid him then upon the well-wrought
> bed,
> And minstrels set by him, to lead the dirge.

(These are supposed to have been the pro-
fessional mourners still common in the
East.)

> So they made moan for him, a doleful lay,
> And in response to them the women wailed.
> White-armed Andromache led the lament,
> While in her hands man-slaying Hector's
> head
> She held: "My husband, young thou'rt
> gone from me,
> And thou hast left me widowed in thy halls.
> And this our boy is but a little child,
> To whom we gave his life, even thou and I
> Ill-fated ones ; nor will he grow, methinks,
> To manhood. Sooner will this town be
> sacked
> Even from its topmost tower ! for thou art
> dead,
> Its warder, who did guard it, and kept safe
> Its noble dames and helpless little ones.

They in the hollow ships will soon set
    forth,"

(that is, as captives and slaves of the victo-
rious Greeks,)

" Myself among them ; and thou, too, my
    child,
Wilt follow me to do unseemly tasks,
For an unfeeling master labouring ;
Or some Achaian will seize thee by the arm
And hurl thee from the tower, — a wretched
    fate, —
Wroth because Hector slew his brother, or
His son, or father ; for at Hector's hands
Full many of the Achaians bit the earth."
(Ibid. 719–738.)

There is a ring of grim exultation even in
the widow's wail.

The later cyclic poets say this prophecy of
Andromache concerning her son's death was
fulfilled ; but they are probably merely accepting the hint here given them. Lovers
of Virgil will recall the scene in Epirus,
seven years later, where Andromache, seeing the boy Ascanius, weeps at the resemblance to his cousin and playfellow, her lost
Astyanax.

"Not gentle was thy father in the fray !
Therefore the people mourn him through the
    town,
But with me most will bitter pain abide !
For thou didst not stretch forth thy hands
    to me,
When dying, from thy bed, nor didst thou
    speak
Some memorable word to me, which I
Would have remembered night and day in
    tears."

So spoke she, wailing, and the women
    moaned,
Responsive ; and among them in her turn
Hecabè then began the loud lament :
" Hector, by far the dearest to my soul
Of all my children !   When thou wert alive
Dear wert thou to the gods, and they indeed
Have cared for thee even in the doom of
    death.
My other sons the fleet Achilles sold,
Those whom he caught, beyond the unrest-
    ing sea,
In Samos, Imbros, Lemnos wrapt in smoke ;
But when with his keen sword he took thy
    life,
Oft did he drag thee round his comrade's
    tomb,

Patroclos' mound, whom thou hadst slain,
     nor yet
Even so did raise him up!"

(Again in Hecabè's words we hear the fierce
exultation of women fit to be the mothers
and wives for a race of savage warriors.)

                    "Now fresh as dew
And fair to see thou liest in thy halls,
Like one whom, smiting with his gentle darts,
Apollo of the silvern bow has slain."
Weeping she spoke, and roused unbounded
     grief.   (*Ibid.* 739–760.)

Artemis or Apollo was thought to have slain
those who died by some sudden and apparently painless death.

The next incident is a most unlooked-for
yet effective one. That Hector's mother
and wife should lament him is to be expected; but what is Helen, that she should
take a leading place in this closing scene?
Yet the pathos of her words fully justifies
the poet's boldness in introducing her
here:—

Then third among them Helen led their
     wail:

K

"O Hector, far the dearest to my soul
Of all thy brethren !   Godlike Alexandros,
Who led me hither, is indeed my husband,—
Would he had perished first !

                         For twenty years
It is already since I hither came,
Leaving my fatherland ; and never yet
An evil word, nor rude, I heard from thee.
If any other in the palace halls
Upbraided me, thy brethren, or their wives
Fair-robed, or sisters, or thy mother,—
    but
Thy sire was ever gentle as a father
To me,"—

(Hecabè evidently had not always shown
the same self-control toward this unwelcome and unwedded daughter-in-law,)

"Yet thou, persuading them with words
Restrained them, with thy gentleness of soul
And gentle words: and so I mourn in grief
For thee, and for my wretched self as well ;
For in wide Troy there is no other one
Kindly or friendly. All men shudder at
    me ! "   (*Ibid.* 761–775.)

Here the long story may fairly be said
to end. There remains only a quiet and
brief description, in thirty lines, of the

ceremonies in Hector's honour. The last line is, —

So they made ready knightly Hector's grave.

It is quite possible that these closing scenes enlist our modern sympathies as they did not the feelings of the Greeks, for example, in the fifth century B.C. Hector is certainly much nearer to our hearts than is his savage foe. And he is, in fact, of all the stately figures in the poem, not only the most pathetic, but also, personally, the most blameless. Achilles fights, like most of the Greek chieftains, for glory, and afterward for revenge. Agamemnon is selfish and rapacious, Menelaos not eminent for courage or strength. Even Priam shares the guilt of Paris, since, but for the old king's infatuated devotion to his sinning son, Helen and the treasure stolen with her would long ago have been restored, liberal atonement made, and the fatal war-cloud averted from the Trojan city. Hector does not uphold Paris in the council-hall. But in the field he fights to the end, though hopeless of success, to defend his dear native city so long as he may. He must fall, to be sure, because he is, as we have said, the bulwark of Ilios, and Ilios must perish for the sin of Paris, which it has made its own.

Yet, in the closing scene, a great poetic genius brings him home, honoured and loved in death above all men, to be lamented by his wife, by his mother, and last of all by Helen, herself the cause of all the misery. Even at this final touch we shall certainly not raise the objection — though the Greek audience might well have done so — that the hero of the poem is forgotten, the champion of the lost and unrighteous cause unduly exalted. Whether the ancient singer intended to suggest it or not, let us hope he would not have repelled the thought with which we close the Iliad: How much happier is Andromache in despairing widowhood, how much more blessed is even Hector in death, than Helen, beautiful still and ever young, destined yet to disarm Menelaos' vengeance by her loveliness, and to return to a prosperous life in Sparta, but surrounded by hate and bitterest scorn, and hearing always within her own heart the voice of self-contempt. Nay, she is even conscious that she and her paramour are to be a "byword among men of a far generation" (VI. 358). This is one of the very few passages where Homer (or one of his folk) seems to glance down the long corridors of time toward ourselves!

IV

THE PLOT OF THE ODYSSEY

THE kinship of Iliad and Odyssey can never be denied. Despite microscopic dissimilarities which have been noted, the dialect, the metre, and, we may add, with reasonable allowance for the difference in subject, even the vocabulary, remain essentially unchanged as we pass from the earlier to the younger epic. Where the same characters appear in both poems, — for example, Odysseus, Nestor, Menelaos, — there is a careful consistency in the traits assigned to them. This statement may be extended even to Achilles, though he appears in the Odyssey only as a ghost in the underworld. The sole important exception, if she be one, is Helen. Even in this case the difference is of course partly one of circumstances ; and the restoration of Menelaos' wife to her former position may have been firmly fixed in the legend before Homer. So Tennyson, with all the changes he permits himself, could perhaps hardly have brought back Guinevere to Arthur's throne, or even bidden Elaine live, to wed happily with Launcelot. We may even please ourselves with the belief that our sterner Teutonic or Keltic morality made the queen's fall from virtue an irreparable one, just as the Greek worship of beauty could hardly be satisfied unless Helen rode, unconquerable still, in all her radiant charms, over the black billows of a war which was aroused by her sin, and had engulfed the chosen youth of her generation!

In what we may call the accidents of structure, also, there are striking analogies between the two Homeric poems. Each deals with the long-delayed but sure and complete fulfilment of a decree uttered by Zeus. In the first book of the Iliad, Thetis prays that the Greeks may suffer in atonement for Achilles' wrongs (508–510), and Zeus impressively nods his assent (524–527). In the assembly of the gods at the opening of the Odyssey, Zeus himself proposes Odysseus' home-return (Book I. 76, 77), and in the similar divine council which opens Book V. declares it as the settled decree of fate (41, 42) : —

"So is it destined that he shall see his be-
    loved, returning
Unto his high-roofed hall and unto the land
    of his fathers."

This divine machinery seems to us, perhaps, a rather foreign and artificial addition to the ancient epic; and in Virgil's age of scepticism it evidently is so, to some extent. But much the same effect is produced, also, upon our minds, at the present day, by the witch scenes in Macbeth. Yet Hecate and her beldames were, probably, three centuries ago, quite as real to many Englishmen as the gods of the Odyssey were to the poet's first auditors. Indeed, we ourselves are hardly far enough removed from Cotton Mather's demonology and the Salem witchcraft to stigmatize either the Homeric theology or Shakespeare's witches as merely a degrading superstition.

As the Iliad opens in the tenth and last year of Troy's beleaguerment, so the companion poem begins with the tenth and final year of Odysseus' long wanderings on his homeward way.   Each epic crowds its action into a comparatively small number of days, —fifty-one in the Iliad, forty-one in the Odyssey, while even of these a few only are eventful, — but both poems give us also, incidentally, vivid pictures of previous events, and significant glimpses as well into the future.   As Achilles' doom was thrice foretold with increasing definiteness, so now we hear of Menelaos' destiny (Odyssey, IV. 561-569), to be transferred, without dying, to the Elysian plain, because he is wedded to Zeus' daughter Helen ; and we listen also to an equally mystical hint as to the hero Odysseus' own last adventure (XI. 134-136) : —

> " And Death shall come to thee out of the
> waters ;
> Gentle shall be his coming to slay thee, when
> thou art wearied,
> Aging slowly, and seeing thy people happy
> about thee."

In the Iliad, we hear only briefly, and as it were accidentally, concerning the origin of the war and its progress hitherto; while four entire books of the younger epic are taken up with the hero's own account of previous adventures. But it must be remembered that the Iliad professes to deal only with an episode, —

Sing, O goddess, *the wrath* of Achilles, —

while the Odyssey is a story with a hero: —

Tell me, O Muse, of *the man* of many de-
    vices, who widely
Wandered, when he had sacked that well-
    walled city of Troia.

So that these four books of narrative (IX.–XII.) are after all no digression, and require no apology.

The device of plunging into the midst of the action, and permitting a leading character to relate his own exploits, has been imitated frequently; for example, closely by Virgil, less so by Milton. Lovers of the Autocrat will remember how the Breakfast Table was once shocked by the remark, "A woman would rather hear a man talk than an angel, any time!" and how it is justified by the citation of a passage in Paradise Lost, where Adam asks from the archangel concerning the deeper mysteries of creation, but Eve withdraws into the garden : —

> "Her husband the relator she preferred
>   Before the Angel."

The magician who told the loves of Othello and Desdemona also realized how effective it is to hear from the hero's own lips the tale

> "of most disastrous chances,
> Of moving accidents by flood and field."

Even the Shakespearean *motif* of woman's love won through sympathy is original with Nausicaa's poet, though Virgil's Dido and her passion make a larger element in the epic plot.

Perhaps it may be added, as another feature of both poems, that the catastrophe is skilfully retarded, and the exact manner in which it will be brought about is long hidden from the listener. As the intervention and death of Patroclos, extinguishing Achilles' wrath in the mightier flame of his grief, could not easily be foreseen, so the trial of strength with the bow, proposed in good faith by Penelope to decide her choice among the suitors, puts a great advantage into her unrecognized husband's hands. Several passages early in the Odyssey, suggesting that young Telemachos may himself destroy the suitors, especially Pallas Athene's own words reminding the prince of Orestes' brave deed (I. 298–302), leave us in some doubt, until his father and he unite their counsels and their valour in the great closing scenes.

Here, however, we perhaps touch upon the chief defect of the Iliad. Its action is retarded by interruptions, not merely by digressions. The Odyssey is 'the shorter poem by several thousand lines, but yet has both a much greater variety of interest and a completer unity. We do not, I think, feel at any time that the action of the Odyssey is deliberately and unduly delayed. While Achilles is unseen and almost forgotten through many books of

the Iliad, we almost never lose sight of
Odysseus, and his fortunes are always
of supreme importance. This single and
unbroken thread of human interest aids
essentially in making the Odyssey what we
believe it is, — the best of all the good
stories that ever were told !

The most striking difference between
the two poems may be found in the un-
varied setting of the elder epic, the shifting scene of the younger. In the Iliad,
our gaze ranges only from the ships and
cabins of the Greeks on the Hellespon-
tine shore to the homes and streets of
the beleaguered town, or at farthest to
Zeus' seat on Ida whence he overlooks
both hosts.   Even the divine abodes seem
close at hand : the gods, debating only upon
the issue of the war, keep their eyes fixed,
as it were, upon the Trojan plain, and
nearly all of them actually enter the field
of battle on some occasion.

In the Odyssey, the heavens are grown
larger as well as more serene, while of the
earth we have an infinitely wider and more
varied view.   First of all, we glance, with

the gods, at Calypso's remote isle, where Odysseus pines in exile. Then, after a vivid glimpse at Ithaca and the suitors' misdeeds, we see Telemachos set off for the kingdoms of the mainland. As Nestor and Menelaos relate to him the story of their homeward voyages from Troyland, they seem to put us for the moment in direct connection with the familiar scene of the Iliad. Again, we follow Odysseus as he starts from Calypso's abode, and, sailing, drifting, swimming, reaches at last the Phæacians' shore. At the banquet, we retrace with him the world-wide wanderings, during which each of his comrades has found a miserable end. Presently, we sway over the long surges with him once more, as he passes homeward, sleeping soundly through the all-night voyage, upon the magic bark that flies " swifter than the thought of man." Meantime, the wanderings of Telemachos and the perplexities of Penelope have occasionally divided our attention. Two-thirds of the poem are completed when father and son are united in the faithful swineherd's cabin. From this point the swiftly moving action is centred in the little island kingdom of Ithaca.

Some great advantages the Odyssey certainly gains through this widening of its scene. The Iliad offers us, as has been said, a single magnificent picture, that of Troy Besieged. Even the Olympian gods seem merely to occupy a coincident upper stage, as in the mediæval miracle-plays heaven and earth, indeed hell also, are represented simultaneously open before the eyes of the audience. Conditions are, so to speak, abnormal, certainly exceptional, everywhere in the Iliad. The Greeks are homeless and demoralized. The camp is full of captive widows and orphaned maids condemned to a state worse than mere slavery. The town is crowded with the armies of its allies, and reduced almost to desperation. The very gods in heaven imitate mankind with unseemly quarrels and threats, or even with actual violence, culminating in the opera-bouffe scene where Hera castigates Artemis. There is no other picture of war so brilliant, so vivid, so indelibly stamped upon the imagination of mankind.

Now, if the younger poem had confined itself to Odysseus' home-coming and grim vengeance on the jackals that troubled the lion's lair, this picture of the impoverished royal family, the disordered palace, and the riotous suitors would have been hopelessly inferior in tragic dignity and in artistic scope to that contest which so long shook the Scamandrian plain, and made Pluto leap from his throne in terror lest his ghastly realm be revealed to the light of the sun. But in the Odyssey, as an adequate compensation, is unrolled the magnificent background, the entire Homeric world.

Through Telemachos' eyes we see Nestor and Menelaos ruling in peace and in luxury over prosperous, contented Greek peoples; and thus we acquire, through contrast, a juster conception of distracted Ithaca, as well as a delightful picture of patriarchal Hellas in times of peace.

In Scheria we have a happy ideal sketch, not without mildly satirical strokes, of a still gentler race.   As sailors and voyagers the Phæacians are beyond rivalry, but otherwise their life is an idle one.   As their merry ruler says,

" Ever delightful to us is the banquet, music
        and dancing,
Garments changed full often, and hot-water
        baths, and our couches."

Evidently a people to be looked upon by Greek eyes with an indulgent smile.

In Odysseus' narrative we have, again, added like a darker fringe to these bright pictures, the wild scenes on the edge of the habitable world.   We shudder in the Cyclops' cave, flee from Scylla's writhing heads, hear the Sirens' song as the waves dash over their victims' whitening bones, and even gain more than a glimpse at the mist-wrapped abode of the dead.

These adventures, also, glorify Odysseus, the chief figure in them all, and accompany him, as it were, toward his desecrated home. As the unknown and oft-insulted beggar rolls grim, silent eyes about the tumultuous hall of his heritage, marking for death the

L

unbidden banqueters, we remember that this is the same dauntless hero who quelled Circe, blinded Polyphemus, and called up Teiresias from Hades. We realize that Pallas and Hermes, who saved him then, will surely make him resistless now.

This poem, then, is an artistic whole; and the key to its unity is truly given in the opening note. It is the personality of Odysseus, the story of his return to Ithaca. And yet we may find that the temptation will at times beset us, even more than with the Iliad, to forget that whole in the dreamy enjoyment of its parts. We may even excuse ourselves with the thought that the poet himself has not wholly resisted the corresponding temptation. The singer of the Odyssey seems to have much more of the romantic spirit than he — or they — of the Iliad. There is an occasional appeal to senti-ment for its own sake. There is a tender and lingering touch in certain episodes, which indicates that they are elaborated for their own idyllic beauty as much as for the benefit of the plot.

In the Iliad, the rare appeals to softer emotions are more evidently for the sake of contrast. Hector's parting, to take a shining example, avowedly foreshadows his death, deepening its pathos and impressiveness. Mighty indeed — so runs the undercurrent of our thought — is Achilles; mightier yet the justice that dooms guilty Ilios, since it could compel the fall even of such a worthy favourite among gods and men as Hector. If we linger a moment over the guilty love of Paris and Helen, we see in the same instant — never in truth more clearly — the wronged and baffled Menelaos, and almost hear the swift wings of his coming revenge. But with Nausicaa we linger not only long, but lovingly. We are forgetting Penelope ; and I fear we might almost find it in our hearts to forgive the sea-worn and war-worn hero if he too had forgotten her !

Still more difficult to fit into the ethical frame of the picture is the Helen of the Odyssey. As she, or her poet, unfolds each womanly and queenly accomplishment, and, touching even upon the dreadful past, manages to recall scenes and motives which soften our feelings as to her abiding in Troy, we realize that upon us, also, the starry eyes of Argive Helen glow resistless. We take our places among her fascinated guests, and no longer wonder that she outlived that terrible night when Priam's gray hairs won no mercy, and Pallas' shrine could not save Cassandra's honour. (There are works of art in which the dagger is seen dropping from Menelaos' hand as Helen unveils before him: for example, Baumeister, pp. 745, 746.) To us, even as to the brother of Antilochos slain and to Odysseus' fatherless son, Helen proffers the nepenthe which drowns just grief and resentment for the evils of former days. Yet all this is at least aside from, if not antagonistic to, the avowed theme and purpose of the poet.

If Nausicaa is lovable as well as loving, it may perhaps be pleaded that she is so much the fitter to be the last temptation of the patient hero, as he passes on, lonely and saddened, yet steadfast, homeward. Calypso, he knows, was fairer and statelier than his mortal wife had ever been. Nausicaa, too, he will gladly honour as a divinity. Yet,

> " East or west,
> Home is best."

But why should Helen be ever beautiful, and honoured, and even happy, while faultless Penelope grows old in sorrow and persecution ? One is tempted to think that our poet has himself failed to see any adequate retribution overtaking his men and women ; that he even, like an earlier Euripides, emphasizes in his art the failure of the divinity to visit vengeance upon sin, and to bestow happiness upon the righteous.

Perhaps it will be wiser, nevertheless, to recur to our former phrase, and to recognize in the Odyssey merely an increasing romantic element, a bolder appeal to sentiment, a fuller elaboration of the parts for the sake of their own beauty. It is a familiar tendency, which the late John Addington Symonds was never tired of pointing out. There will always be more of us to enjoy Praxiteles' softened outlines than Phidias' rugged strength. " Euripides the

human " draws tears more easily than
Æschylos, — or, in more modern terms,
The Vicar of Wakefield more easily than
Macbeth, — though perhaps not from such
deep sources, mysterious even to ourselves.
A more fruitful comparison, however, may
be made with the austere art of Milton and
the linkèd sweetness of Tennyson.

Three thousand years hence, if all other
literature and tradition of England shall
have perished, men may seriously discuss
whether one poet could have composed
Paradise Lost and the Idylls of the King.
The theology of the two is not irreconcila-
ble. The language, the metre, the poetic
tradition, may then appear essentially identical. Certainly, the later poem should
reveal a perfect familiarity with the earlier
one, since the laureate counted as chief
among his masters the " God-gifted organ
voice of England."

So much, at least, is true of Iliad and
Odyssey. It is not strange that the claim
of Homer as the author of both was main-
tained among the ancients, even after the
Cyclic epics and the Homeric hymns had

been rightly assigned to a later age and to
feebler hands. There are still many who
find it easier to abide by the tradition of
one great epic poet than to accept the possibility of two so alike and so equal in power.
And surely it is conceivable that a single
genius should have shaped the two great
poems. Tennyson's poetical career lasted
just about as long as the period from the
composition of the earliest extant drama of
Æschylos which can be accurately dated,
The Persians, to the death of Euripides
and Sophocles. A briefer epoch might include both Homeric epics. The Iliad and
the Odyssey may to many seem more closely
akin than In Memoriam and Harold. I
find it, for myself, however, in high degree
improbable that one man lived to see, and
even led, so great a transition from classic
toward romantic taste ; from an age which
was content to devote an Iliad to the glori-
fication of war to the generation which felt
the full pathos of Odysseus' longing for
home and rest, overpowering even the
charm of world-wide adventure and marvellous experience. Such a transition is

implied in the ancient belief that the Iliad was the work of Homer's prime, the Odyssey the child of his age. Though perhaps not literally, it is figuratively true, — true of a race, of a civilization, if not of an individual.

The argument that it is easier to believe in the existence of one great epic poet than of two, or of a school, seems to us distinctly against the weight of evidence. It is not a mere popular fancy that arranges the greatest authors in contemporary groups. Horace is the natural pendant of Virgil, Schiller and Lessing help to render Goethe's career intelligible, Lowell was produced by the conditions which made Emerson possible. The best illustration is, however, the age of Greek drama. Even the three tragedians just mentioned did not hold the field alone. If Phrynichos, Ion, Agathon, and the rest had survived, we might perhaps have accepted the Athenian people's judgment, which repeatedly preferred them to the surviving masters, granting to Œdipus the King only a second prize, and to Medea the third ! Even so, there are yet remaining beautiful though scanty epic fragments, indicating that there may have been not merely two, but twenty, great masters of the hexameter.

Before we turn to the somewhat detailed discussion of the structure of the Odyssey, I should like to dwell for an instant on the contrast in the spirit of the two glorious epics. The prevailing note of the Iliad seems to be the fierce delight in strife and bloodshed. The war-worn and wave-worn hero of the Odyssey realizes that he has gained rich experience and wisdom by wandering, and his eagerness to see and know is not easily sated; yet the chord which vibrates most strongly throughout the younger poem is the longing for the peace of home-life.

There is a passage near the close of the Odyssey in which the night following the slaying of the suitors is divinely prolonged, that Odysseus may enjoy with Penelope comfort and repose after twenty years' separation. The poet has taken this opportunity to recall rapidly, through Odysseus' lips, in their proper sequence, the adventures of his hero since the fall of Troy. We may seize the same occasion to pass in review some of the familiar tales of folk-lore which have crystallized about the central story of the returning husband.

Little success in winning popular approval has attended the efforts spent in attacking the essential unity of plot and of probable authorship in our Odyssey. Yet for every comedy of Shakespeare, save The Tempest, suggestions have been found in earlier works, usually in tales of other races. Even so, it is no detraction from Homer's originality if many incidents woven into the Odyssey are traced to myths unconnected with Penelope's husband, some of them probably not even Greek in their origin.

The verses of Homer outlining the narrative as it was thus told to Penelope will serve, at least in part, as texts for us to gloss.

First Odysseus told how he the Cicones
    conquered.   (Od. XXIII. 310.)

These allies of Priam furnish the only victory and booty of the Ithacans in the long tale of woe and death. Even here defeat quickly followed, and loss of many lives.

Then in the fertile land of the lotus-eaters
        he tarried.   (*Ibid.* 311.)

We are perhaps not yet beyond the pale of realities, and the lotus has been identified sometimes with the "jujuba" of northern Africa; sometimes, also, with the "mandrakes" which Reuben brought to his mother Leah (Genesis xxx. 14). Some narcotic is doubtless indicated by the poetic account, though Homer does not distinctly assert anything more than that Odysseus' comrades liked it : —

Whoso among them the honey-sweet fruit
        of the lotus had tasted
Would not depart from the land, nor even
        report with the tidings.
There were they fain to remain with the
        folk that ate of the lotus,
Feeding ever thereon ; and the path of return was forgotten. (Od. IX. 94–97.)

The incident is a brief and unimportant

one in Homer, and Tennyson's genius may fairly be said to have wrested the subject from the master's hand.

All that the Cyclops wrought he related;
    and how he exacted
Vengeance for comrades brave, by the mon-
    ster ruthlessly eaten.
           (Od. XXIII. 312–313.)

In this case, Odysseus confesses, his companions were more wisely cautious than he. His foolhardy lingering in the cavern till the giant should return is hardly offset by the final escape with a remnant of his crew. Perhaps these features mark the story as an imperfect adaptation from a foreign source. The legend of the one-eyed man-eating ogre is curiously widespread, from Tartary to Ireland. It is, at any rate, fitted skilfully into the Homeric plot; for Poseidon, we are told, is the Cyclops' father, and the sea-god's wrath follows relentlessly the men who had blinded his son. Yet, as in Coleridge's tale of the albatross, the chief guilty one — if guilt there was in such self-defence — is the sole survivor at last!

Æolus, who is next visited, and who gives the winds to Odysseus in a bag, is, according to Andrew Lang, " an heroic ancestor of the witches who down to the present century sold winds in the same fashion to Scottish mariners." These Homeric blasts were, however, the winds that were *not to blow.* Only the west wind was left free, and would have wafted the exiles speedily home. The untying of the sack while Odysseus sleeps recalls the *motif* of the Pandora myth, and of countless others in all lands.

The cannibal Læstrygonians, whom the Ithacans next visit, destroy all the ships save one, with their crews. These savages live by a narrow fiord between high rock walls, where " the paths of day and night are nigh together," and " a sleepless man might earn a double wage " as herdsman. This is surely a reminiscence of the long arctic day. If it is too early a date for Mediterranean sailors to have fared so far as Norway, the vague legend may have reached Greek lands by the overland trade route along which amber came to the southern peoples.

The lonely floating island of Æolus, it has been suggested, may have originated in some sailor's tale of an iceberg. It seems to be near the Læstrygonians' coast, since no night is mentioned as intervening on the voyage from their land to Æolia, and an old tradition made Æolus' wife one of their people.

> Then he related the craft and the many
> devices of Circe.   (Od. XXIII. 321.)

The ethical interpretation of the Circean myth — that sensuality makes men truly bestial — is at least as old as Socrates. But the marvel is doubtless more ancient than the moral. The legend has plenty of parallels elsewhere, the most familiar being Queen Labè in the Arabian Nights, who also transforms her discarded lovers into various beasts. Indeed, the change to animal forms is one of the most familiar elements of enchantment everywhere. The terrible were-wolf superstition died late and hard, if it is even now extinct.

From Circe's island Odysseus made his excursion to Hades, and returned thence to the enchantress. The Kimmerian land of ghosts, ever wrapped in fog, may be a sort of pendant to the Læstrygonian legend, suggested by the long night of the far north or of the far south.

A curious geographical question arises at this point. At Æolus' isle Odysseus was west of his Grecian home, since Zephyrus was to carry him thither. Circe's island, like Læstrygonia, seems to be within a day's sail of Æolus. Yet the hero is said to return from the realm of the dead (Od. XII. 3, 4) to Circe, coming

Unto the isle Ææa, where early Dawn has
        her dwelling :
There are her dancing-places, the land of
        the sun's uprising.

Commentators, old and new, have struggled with the problem how Circe's island home can be both in the remote west and in the far east. President Warren utilizes this passage as the corner-stone of his theory that Homer was aware of the shape of our globe, and makes his hero circumnavigate it. This is but a part of the learned and elaborately woven argument by which Dr. Warren locates the lost earthly Paradise at the north pole. It does not seem quite impossible that a truer cosmology than the later classic beliefs may have been included among those Lost Arts with which Wendell Phillips' silvery tongue delighted our boyhood.

> Then did he tell how he heard the song of
> the clear-voiced Sirens.
>
> (Od. XXIII. 326.)

Their voices are still heard across every "perilous sea of fairyland forlorn." The Wandering Rocks, between which no ship save Argo had ever passed uncrushed, are said to be described in old sailors' tales even among the Aztecs of our own continent. Scylla's writhing heads, each of which drags a man from the vessel's deck, seems to be a polypus or devil-fish. The belief that these creatures are occasionally so enormous as to attack even a ship successfully is by no means only an ancient one.

Lastly, for devouring the sacred kine of Helios, the sun-god, in Thrinakia, the crew of Odysseus' ship are destroyed in a deep-sea shipwreck by Zeus' thunderbolt. The hero, alone, drifts, after many days, to the isle of Calypso, in the centre of the sea. In this lovely earthly Paradise (as Dr. Warren declares it to be, though but a dim and distorted wraith of the true tradition remains, according to him, in Homer) Odysseus spends seven years with the gentle and loving nymph. Of the hero's last voyage, to Phæacia, we have spoken, and shall speak again.

The night-long slumber on the Phæacian ship, already mentioned, seems a clear reminder that the curtain of fairyland is here pushed aside, while the Ithacan wanderer emerges again into the real world. From the Cyclops to the Phæacians, everything lies at an unknown distance from Greece, in a trackless sea, quite beyond the pale of merely human experience. Several passages remind us to include the gentle Phæacians, also, in this part of the tale. We are informed that they were formerly neighbours of the Cyclops, and are "very near to the Immortals." After they have conducted the crafty Ithacan homeward, Poseidon resolves to turn the offending vessel to stone, and wall up their city behind a mountain. The Phæacian king sees the significance of all this, the more as it fulfils an ancient oracle, and bids his people

> "Cease from the convoy of men, when any
> shall come to our city."
>
> (Od. XIII. 180.)

The poetic significance of this passage is surely no less clear. Never shall mariner or adventurer bring further tidings home from the happy Phæacian land. Like the German maiden in the cursed village of Germelshausen, the loving Nausicaa is seen but for a day; nor may any weaker hand "the lost clue regain."

The latter half of the poem has a comparatively realistic character. The scene is either in the great house of Odysseus, or in the swineherd's cabin on the further side of rocky Ithaca. In the accounts of Penelope's and Telemachos' movements, of the suitors' banquets, and finally of the great massacre, many architectural details are incidentally given. So judicious a scholar as Professor Jebb joins in the attempt to piece these together into a scientific restoration of the prehistoric Greek country-house. The results do not seem very fruitful or well assured. But such studies are stimulated and aided by the brilliant discoveries of early architecture in Tiryns, Mykenæ, Troy, and elsewhere. They are certainly wiser and safer than any attempt to illustrate prehistoric customs or manners from the scenes of these books. Thus, on three different occasions a handy missile is thrown at the supposed beggar, Odysseus: Book XVII. 462, a stool, which hits his shoulder; XVIII.394, another footstool, which misses him, but hits the cupbearer; XX. 299, an ox-foot, which is dodged, and strikes the wall. This is an illustration — of what? Surely, only of drunken and lawless manners everywhere; though it also serves to harden Odysseus' heart against all thought of mercy, and perhaps has a grim irony as we think of the deadlier missiles which will so soon hurtle through the shadowy hall in return.

But a loftier tragic tone is felt through

the twenty-second book in particular,
wherein the slaughter of the suitors is
accomplished. Only the minstrel and the
herald, who had served in the hall under
compulsion, are spared. The unfaithful
maid servants, whom the suitors had be-
guiled, are made to clear the hall of their
lovers' bodies, and then are hung, all a-row,
in the courtyard ! Such are the tidings that
are brought by the old nurse, Eurycleia,
to Penelope upon her waking. That she
is long incredulous, and also proves the
stranger, craftily, before she believes him
to be her long-absent lord, troubles Telemachos, and has offended some commentators ; but it only wins a smile from the
man of many wiles himself, who has evidently chosen wisely a wife after his own
heart.

It is in this palace, where the groans of
the dying suitors have hardly died away,
that Odysseus receives again into his arms,
after twenty years' separation, the wife of
his youth. A pathetic touch is the mention of Teiresias' prophecy, indicating that
long wanderings still remain before the

brief space of peaceful old age which is to close the storm-tossed heroic life. Even now his rest is troubled by a weighty care: the death-feud with the kin of the slain suitors. Odysseus cannot refrain from mentioning this, also, in Penelope's hearing, to the boyish son whom this day's work has made a man and a warrior.

"Even he who has slain but a single man in the country,
Though he have left not many thereafter to be his avengers,
Flees into exile, leaving his kin and the land of his fathers.
We have slain these youths, who by far were in Ithaca noblest;
They were the stay of the city: and this I bid thee consider!"
(Od. XXIII. 118–122.)

Odysseus evidently realizes that he has a worse than Corsican vendetta to face. Telemachos' reply naturally expresses the fullest confidence in his father's resources. We would gladly have heard an added word of confidence in the divine aid, which Pallas should have taught him ere now.

With the close of this day the ancient Alexandrian critics believed that the genuine Odyssey ended. But Mr. Lang is no doubt right in reminding us emphatically that no hearer in the heroic age could have been content unless a solution for the feud of blood was added. This is more convincing than his similar assertion that the poet of the Iliad could not have left Hector unburied. Artistically, however, anything that follows the death of the wooers and the happy reunion of the royal pair must seem to us an anti-climax. Furthermore, our attention is unexpectedly distracted by the form which this continuation, the present twenty-fourth book, actually takes. There are, in fact, three nearly distinct pictures making up this closing canto.

First, the scene is transferred, without warning, to the underworld once more, and we overhear a conversation between the ghosts of Agamemnon and Achilles. The latter, for some reason not indicated, now hears for the first time the story of his own funeral in the Troad. It is a stately pageant that is here described, and the glimpse accorded us of the lovely Thetis and her great grief alone rewards us for its perusal. But this is a strange place in which to find it. It could certainly have been made more effective in the eleventh book.

Then follows Odysseus' visit with Telemachos to the upland farm, and the loving recognition of him by his old father and the thralls. Part of this, again, is noble poetry, and we cannot feel that it is precisely out of place, though we certainly do not feel that it is essential to the epic plot. It is, rather, like a sentimental one-act drama or idyl by itself.

Lastly, the kin of the slain take to arms, and are seen approaching the farm. Old Laertes determines to "tilt it out among the lads," and is not, like the father of Tennyson's prince, dissuaded therefrom. A remark of his is really the one stirring word in the scene : —

"Now what a day is this, dear gods! I
    truly am happy,
Seeing my son and my son's son vie with
    each other in valour!"

(Od. XXIV. 514, 515.)

The passage reminds us vaguely of the pictures, popular a few years ago, representing four generations of German imperial stock. Laertes is the only one who kills his man. The victim is the leader of the avengers, and father of the most insolent among the suitors. Then Zeus stays the skirmish with a thunderbolt, and we are told in curt words that Pallas Athene reconciled the feud, at her father's bidding, taking on therefor the guise of mortal Mentor. But not one word of hers is actually reported, and the book ends tamely ; even, as it seems, hastily and lamely.

Perhaps, as Mr. Lang says, such a divine intervention was about the only solution possible, at least without further waste of life. But if the master poet of the Odyssey composed the last two hundred lines in their present form, he was very weary, either of his art altogether or else of this theme. There are few even of the greatest artists who understand the divine art of leaving off betimes. Perhaps the most effective verse in all Dante is that quiet word of Francesca:—

" Quel giorno più non vi leggemmo avanti."

Something may always be left to the imagination of the sympathetic reader.

But as we look back upon the whole mass of Greek epic, upon the Iliad and the Odyssey together, how complete, and how magnificent, is the picture which they create! We must, I think, concede the truth of one of the boldest assertions made by the brilliant and canny Scot who is so often quoted, and still oftener drawn upon, in this essay: If we were forced to lose either Homer or all Greek literature beside, we should hesitate as long as possible ; but at last we should cling to Homer, who anticipates so much that is best in all the other Hellenic poets, and whose world seems to have a completeness and a perfect beauty of its own to which its very remoteness adds a final charm.

" Why floats the amaranth in eternal
        bloom
O'er Ilium's turrets and Achilles' tomb?

> Why lingers fancy where the sunbeams
>   smile
> On Circe's gardens and Calypso's isle ?
> Why follows memory to the gate of Troy
> Her plumed defender and his trembling
>   boy ? ''

The truest answer to his own question Dr. Holmes himself gives in another connection : —

> '' The classic days, those mothers of ro-
>   mance,
>   That roused a nation for a woman's glance;
>   The age of mystery with its hoarded power,
>
>   .   .   .   .   .   .
>
>   Have past and faded like a dream of
>   youth.''

And these tragic yet sweetest memories of the world's lost youth are bound up forever under the rubric that bears the doubted and denied, yet ever glorious name of Homer.

V

THE HOMERIC UNDERWORLD

THE clear voices of inspired poets and philosophers come to us like the cries of the warders high above us on the watch-towers of life. In the dust and turmoil of daily existence, we perchance forget to ask ourselves what are the real goals toward which our efforts tend. Every true poet answers humanity's cry : —

> " To tell the purport of our pain,
> And what our silly joys contain,
> Come, poet, come ! "

It is a lingering instinct, also, which men might be saddened wholly to relinquish, that these same lofty watchers may, perhaps, catch a clearer glimpse than we, even of that which is within the veil. We may be tempted to cry to them, as dear faces vanish from our side : —

" Where are now those silent hosts ?
Where the camping-ground of ghosts ? "

Æschylos' Darius, Virgil's Anchises, Hamlet's ghostly father, speak, as it were, in a voice deeper than the poet's own, of the abode from which they have issued.

In recalling the conceptions of the future life which the Homeric epics shadow forth, we may make an especial effort to solicit their answers to a question which almost every man sometimes asks himself : Do our dead know what is occurring in this world ?

In the crowded battle scenes of the Iliad there is hardly an instant to think of the dead.   When a warrior fell,

The soul, at the wound that was stricken,
Darted hastily forth, as the darkness cov-
    ered his eyelids,
                    (Il. XIV. 518, 519.)

and straightway

Leaving his limbs, to the dwelling of Hades
    his soul had departed,
Sorrowing over his doom, so bereft of his
    youth and his vigour.
                    (Il. XVII. 856, 857.)

As the youthful hero Achilles rides forth to his last great victory, he clearly sees the black shadow of his own death across the pathway ; but when even his steed is endowed with speech to give him a final warning, he only silences sternly the loving voice of prophecy, and plunges the more fiercely into the fray.

" Why foretellest thou, Xanthos, my death ?
     It in nowise is fitting.
Well do I know of myself that I here am
     appointed to perish,
Far from my mother and father beloved :
     yet surely I therefore
Never will cease, till I give to the Trojans
     surfeit of battle."
Speaking, he urged with a shout his hard-
     hoofed horses to vanward.
               (Il. XIX. 420–424.)

When we catch any glimpses of a future existence, they are but the crudest fancies of a savage, fearless, yet life-loving race of warriors. The dead must share the delight in prompt vengeance wreaked upon the foe.

" Verily not unavenged is Asios lying:
     and even

> While he to Hades fareth, the Warder stern
>   of the portal,
> He in his heart shall exult, because I have
>   sent him an escort!"
>
> (Il. XIII. 414–416.)

Food, animals, and captives, are sacrificed upon the funeral pyre, as if earthly needs, and perhaps even the mastery of slaves, might continue in the land of shadows. Our chief passage on this point is Patroclos' funeral (Il. XXIII. 170, etc.).

The body, not the fleeting soul, is oftenest spoken of as the man himself: notably in the very opening lines of the Iliad : —

> Many a hero's soul was hurried untimely to
>   Hades :
> *They themselves* were rendered the booty
>   of dogs and of vultures. . . .

Hades has not yet received his epithet of *Pluto* (lord of wealth), but is, naturally enough, the unpitying, inexorable tyrant, most detested of all divinities.

> . . . Not to be moved, and merciless,
>   truly, is Hades :
> Therefore among all gods is he most hated
>   of mortals.   (Il. IX. 158, 159.)

In the pause of the action around Patroclos slain, there is for the first time space
upon the scene for the soul of the departed.
If the phrase be not too modern, we may say
that Achilles is chastened by suffering, and
learns in his bereavement and grief to think
more deeply and earnestly of the future.
As he lay heavily sleeping, in the night after
the slaying of Hector, upon the lonely shore,

Then unto him there came the soul of
    unhappy Patroclos,
Like in every way to himself when living,
    in stature,
Eyes, and voice, and even the garb that
    covered his body.
Over his head he took his stand, and thus
    he addrest him :
"Art thou asleep, and wert thou forgetful
    of me, O Achilles,
Now that I am dead, who in life wast never
    neglectful ?
Bury me now, in haste, that I pass by the
    portal of Hades.'
Now am I banished afar by the souls, the
    ghosts of the perished.
They forbid me beyond the River among
    them to mingle.

Vainly I wander about by the wide-wayed
    dwelling of Hades.
Give me, I pray thee in sorrow, thy hand :
    for again from the Unseen
Never may I return, when of fire my meed
    thou accordest.
Never as living men may we sit, apart from
    our comrades,
Weaving our counsel : for me hath yawned
    that destiny grievous
Which at the very hour of my birth for me
    was appointed.
Even for you, O Achilles like to the gods, it
    is fated
Here to meet your death, by the wall of the
    valorous Trojans.
Let my bones be laid not apart from thine,
    O Achilles,
But together, as we together were reared in
    the palace. . . .
So may the bones of us twain in a single
    coffer be hidden. . . ."

                (Il. XXIII. 65–91.)

The passage is full of suggestions. The
shape of Patroclos, we learn, is still the
same as in life. His love is unaltered ; his
eagerness to share even the urn that hides
Achilles' bones is a powerful tribute to

friendship. Especially pitiful is it, that he
fancies he can still clasp the hand of the
living. Patroclos — that is, his poet — is
a fatalist. Man's doom is fixed from his
birth. (A similar utterance of Hector
will be remembered.) Patroclos' prophetic
knowledge of Achilles' death is an enlarge-
ment of his living powers. The surviving
friend is astonished, even in his dream, at
his friend's return, but promises obedience
in all, adding : —

" Yet draw closer to me, till so for a mo-
      ment embracing
Each the other, we sate ourselves with bit-
      ter lamenting."
Even as thus he spoke, his affectionate arms
      he extended,
Yet did he clasp him not: but under the
      earth like a smoke-wraith
Wailing hurried the soul.
              In amaze updarted Achilles,
Smote together his hands, and thus did he
      speak in his sorrow.
" Ah me ! So then even in Hades' dwell-
      ing remaineth
Still the soul and phantom : but bodily life
      is departed.

N

> All night long at my side did the soul of
>   unhappy Patroclos
> Stand. . . ."   (*Ibid.* 97–106.)

Achilles, then, who perhaps until now had hardly given an earnest thought thereto, gains from this vision a conviction that there is indeed a life beyond death.

This visit of Patroclos, however, was possible only because the funeral rites are yet incomplete. When once his body is burned, the soul will cross the river, and revisit the living no more. (*Charon* seems to be a post-Homeric figure; cf. Eustathios, 166, 6. 36, and Pausanias, X. 28. 2, who quotes the earliest mention of Charon known, from the post-Homeric " Minyas.")

Whether Patroclos will still be aware, in the spirit world, of what is passing on earth, Achilles does not know, nor does the poet, apparently. When the body of Hector is surrendered for burial, at Priam's entreaty, Achilles apostrophizes his lost friend : —

> " Be not wroth, O Patroclos, at me, if, in
>   Hades abiding,

Thou shalt learn that I have rendered illus-
    trious Hector
Back to his loving father: for fitting the
    ransom he offered,
Wherefrom I upon thee will bestow such
    share as is seemly."
(Il. XXIV. 593–595.)

Perhaps the mere fact of Hector's arrival
beyond the River will convey the knowledge
to Patroclos. No response to this appeal
ever comes to Achilles, and the pages of the
Iliad tell us nothing more as to his friend's
condition or knowledge in the other life.

The chief Homeric passages in regard to
the world of the dead, however, occur in
the Odyssey. The connection of Odysseus'
voyage to Hades with the general plot of
the poem was mentioned in the last chapter.
Circe sends Odysseus thither, to consult
the blind prophet Teiresias, who there, as
on earth, is the only one who truly sees,
with the eyes of wisdom and prophecy.
That is, he is a prophet not because he is
dead, but in spite of being dead. And to
Circe's isle the Ithacan with his crew returns.

This is the strangest, and the remotest, of all the adventures with which the hero regaled the Phæacian banqueters. On other occasions the truth hardly falls from Odysseus' lips unmixed with cunning falsehoods. As Virgil dismisses Æneas from the underworld through the ivory gate, the portal of untruthful visions, so modern men may prefer to read the voyage to Kimmeria merely as the romancing Tale of an Ancient Mariner.

The old sailor voices our own surprise at the very first mention of the subject. When Circe commands the dread pilgrimage, he exclaims in terrified astonishment:—

"Who, I pray thee, O Circe, upon this
        voyage may guide us?
Never a man ere this in a black ship journeyed to Hades!"

(Od. X. 501, 502.)

We did not expect to seek the spirit world beyond the sea. The conception of a Hades beneath our feet had been made familiar to us by one of the most striking passages in the Iliad. In a fierce battle scene, in which the gods also take part, Homer declares:—

Then Aidoneus, monarch of those below,
    was affrighted.
Startled, he leaped from his throne and
    shouted, for fear that above him
Cloven the world should be by the stout
    earth-shaker, Poseidon.
So unveiling his realm to the eyes of men
    and immortals:
— Ghastly, afar extended, that even of gods
    is detested!   (Il. XX. 61–65.)

There is also a solemn form of invocation
used in oaths, which sounds as if it was,
even in the poet's day, an ancient tradi-
tional formula. In it Aidoneus and Persephone are thus referred to: —

Thou, O Sun, who all things seest, and
    everything hearest,
Rivers also, and Earth, and ye, the twain
    that beneath us
Punish the forceless men, whoso have sworn
    to a falsehood.   (Il. I. 277–279.)

Is Persephone's meadow of asphodel, then,
on the earth's surface, or beneath it? The
difficulty is a real one. It has usually met
with an explanation which is not a solution
at all; viz., that Homer, or the various

authors of the poems, had two worlds of the dead, or two conceptions as to the abode of the departed, and either never noticed the inconsistency in the two sets of allusions, or at any rate never made any attempt to harmonize them.

Dr. Warren's theory is fully expounded in his learnèd book, Paradise Found. According to him, Homer conceived the world as a globe, inhabited only in the northern hemisphere. Okeanos, or the River of Ocean, is a circular current, belting the globe like the torrid zone of modern charts, though not so wide. Across this stream Odysseus sails to Kimmeria, on the southern or under side of the earth, and so actually *under us*, as Australia is under us, yet still upon the surface of our world.

This is not wholly unlike the Dantesque conception of Purgatory. Dante's Inferno is a funnel, beginning just under Jerusalem, and gradually narrowing to the centre of the earth, where Lucifer is forever held fast. At the time when Lucifer's fall created this funnel, an exactly similar cone of earth was forced out at the antipodes, thus forming

the lofty Purgatorial mountain. The swift
voyage of Dante's saved sinners, from Tiber's
mouth to the shore of this far southern hill,
reminds us — though it is probably a purely
accidental coincidence — of the quick passage from Circe's isle to the dim shore of
Kimmeria. Homer plainly says that the
north wind is to bear them thither. In
fact, Dr. Warren's hypothesis accounts for
the statements of Homer more clearly than
any other, — if other there be. In my own
mind I vacillate between accepting it, and
incredulity as to Homer's having any clear
geometrical ideas and theories at all. Dr.
Warren bases his arguments upon his firm
belief in an original, full, divine revelation
of cosmic truth to man. Fragments of this
forfeited truth, gradually dimmed and distorted with lapse of time, are traceable, he
believes, in the earliest traditions and myths
of many races. But President Warren's
Homeric theories do not, necessarily, stand
and fall with his creed of an original Eden,
and of primeval wisdom granted to man
far surpassing all our modern knowledge.

Upon the farther shore of ocean Odysseus digs a shallow trench, and fills it with honey, milk, wine, water, and the blood of sacrificed sheep. This is the ordinary food in life, and needed here to give the ghosts strength to know Odysseus and to speak audibly. Odysseus holds converse with them in turn, across the trench.

A foolish young companion of Odysseus, Elpenor by name, had broken his neck by a fall, when half-drunk, from Circe's palace roof just before Odysseus started. His soul had preceded his comrades on their rushing voyage. He is first to address them. This he can do, even without drinking from the trench, because, as in the case of Patroclos, his body still lies unburied. Old Bishop Eustathios, wordiest of commentators, remarks that Elpenor is foolish in death as in life, demanding that Odysseus return to Ææa and erect for him a funeral mound on the shore of that utterly untravelled sea! Odysseus agrees, very curtly, to this unreasonable and useless task. The artistic purpose in this episode is, no doubt, to emphasize the rapidity of the soul's passage to Hades.

Next, the ghost of the hero's mother chances to hover near, unconscious of her son's presence. Though he weeps piteous tears at the sight, he holds her, like the rest aloof from the trench, as he is bidden, until Teiresias first approaches. Even he fears the hero's drawn sword, and dares not quaff at the trenchside until it is safely sheathed. Then the dark blood revives his strength, and he tells Odysseus in outline all his future adventures, not merely those of his home-coming, but the long later wanderings, his brief peaceful old age, and the death that shall come to him " out of the waters." This is the prophecy which Odysseus repeated, as will be remembered, to Penelope.

Then Odysseus asks the seer how his mother may know him, and is told that she must be permitted to drink at the trench.

> " Then did my mother
> Come and drink of the darksome blood, and instantly knew me,
> Sorrowing then with wingèd words she spoke and addressed me :
> How have you come, my child, down under the shadowy darkness,

You, who still are alive? 'Tis a terrible
    sight for the living.
Are you but just come hither, as you from
    the Troad have wandered
Long with your vessel and comrades? And
    Ithaca did you not visit?
Have you not seen as yet the wife who
    dwells in your palace?"

            (Od. XI. 152–162.)

This passage may fairly be said to answer, so far as Homer is concerned, our question as to the knowledge possessed by the departed. If any love can bridge the gulf of worlds, and see through the veil of death, it must surely be the love of motherhood. Yet she does not even know her living son, until the natural feebleness of her ghost-nature is re-enforced by the draught of blood: and then her first words show that she has known nothing of his adventures since they parted. To be sure, she answers his inquiries about affairs in Ithaca with full knowledge. But that need only show that she has recently died. Her husband, old Laertes, is still living in a hale old age when Odysseus reaches Ithaca again, some

eight years later. The mother had pined
away, she tells him, purely for longing to
see him, her absent son.

Here the *motif* of the Iliad is repeated
with a deeper pathos, when Odysseus thrice
attempts in vain to clasp his mother's form,
and cries out

" Mother mine, why tarry you not as I long
        to embrace you ?   .
So were we clasped in the arms of each
        other, even in Hades :
Then might both of us sate our thirst for
        bitter lamenting !
Or but a phantom alone has lofty Per-
        sephone sent me ?"   (*Ibid.* 210-213.)

But the mother assures him : —

"Nay but this is the nature of mortals,
        when they have perished.
Flesh no longer, and bones, are held by the
        sinews together.
They by the forceful might of the flaming
        fire are vanquished,
Even as soon as the breath from the white
        bones takes its departure.
Then as a dream man's soul goes fluttering
        forth, and has vanished."
                        (*Ibid.* 218-222.)

Even the shades of the greatest heroes are equally helpless. Agamemnon, lord of men, must drink of the blood before he can recognize his old comrade, and then he too makes a vain attempt to embrace him. Agamemnon asks after his only son, adding :—

> "Not yet, surely, on earth has perished
> royal Orestes."   (*Ibid.* 461.)

Perhaps this confidence is simply because the young prince has not joined his kin in Hades; for Agamemnon is wandering about sorrowfully, in the company of those slain with him by his treacherous wife on the day of his home-coming. Of the son Odysseus can tell him nothing.

The most famous episode in this book, however, is the conversation with the ghost of Achilles. Seeing him approach, still surrounded by his illustrious friends, — Ajax and Patroclos and Nestor's son Antilochos, —Odysseus hails him as one honoured like a god in life, and still a mighty ruler among the shades. But Achilles replies :—

> "Speak not comforting words of death, O
> noble Odysseus.

Verily I would choose to live as the serf of
    another,
Even a needy man, who had but a scanty
    subsistence,
Than to be sovereign here of all who are
    dead and departed."
(Ibid. 488–491.)

He, too, asks after his son, and also as to
the aged father in whose name Priam had
appealed to his pity after Hector's [death.
And our last glimpse of him is as he

Passes with mighty strides across the as-
    phodel meadow,
Happy because I had called his son an illus-
    trious warrior.   (Ibid. 539–540.)

The latter portion of the eleventh book,
describing the punishment of Tantalos, Sisy-
phos, and other mythic heroes of a still
earlier age, is generally believed to be an
addition by a later hand, and is certainly
not easily harmonized with the picture of
Odysseus sitting beside the trench, com-
muning with the throng of flitting ghosts.
The passage does not vitally modify our
general sketch, however. The most striking figure in it is Heracles, who appears

here as a mere soulless *eidolon*, since his real self — that is, no doubt, his soul, perhaps inhabiting a celestial body —

> Among the immortals of Heaven
> Taketh delight in the feast, and to graceful
> Hebè is wedded.   (*Ibid.* 602–603.)

It would appear that ordinarily the invisible soul, *psyche*, passing from the dead body to the land of shades, was immediately invested with an *eidolon*, a likeness of its former body, which could be seen and recognized even by living men. It is, however, plain that this existence was a most aimless and limited one. In spite of Plato's stern rebuke of this passage as making men cowardly in the face of death, we can hardly wonder, under such conditions, at Achilles' disconsolate words. The prehistoric Greeks were too happy in life, too closely attached to outward nature, too fully in possession of a harmonious development of body and mind, to form any very vivid conception of a continued existence for the soul after its departure from the body. Indeed this statement would apply almost as well to the Athenians, with the important exception of Plato himself, who in this, as in so much else, seems rather under Oriental than Hellenic influence. To him the body is indeed the prison-house of the soul.

The beginning of the last book in the Odyssey has been regarded by the critics, from Aristarchos down, as one of the latest additions to the poem.   With the exception, however, of a greater dignity imparted to Achilles and Agamemnon, the scene does not contradict the conception formed from reading the eleventh book. It is noteworthy that the difficulty about the location of the spirit world remains to the last. In the opening account of the soul's passage to Hades there is no hint of a descent.

Hermes the Helper along the watery ways
          did lead them :
Past Oceanus' streams and the White Rock
          now they were hurried.
Helios' gate they passed, and the land of
          visions was traversed.
Presently they had entered within the as-
          phodel meadow,

Where are abiding the souls, the ghosts of
    men that have perished.

(Od. XXIV. 10–14.)

Nevertheless the closing words of the scene
are

. . . So did they speak to each other,
Standing in Hades' halls under earth's mys-
    terious regions.   (*Ibid.* 203–204.)

In Virgil's time the commoner conception
of an " underworld " was too fully fixed, or
the actual geography too well known, to
venture upon sending his hero on such a
voyage, and accordingly Æneas lands and
enters a cavern. Dante found it necessary
to avoid altogether the question of the actual point where the underworld is entered.
He merely says : —

" I found myself within a wood obscure."

Thus farther and ever farther into dimmer
distance recedes, as we journey from the
dawn, the cloud-hung gate of Wonder-
land !

<h1 style="text-align:center">VI</h1>

ODYSSEUS AND NAUSICAA

AMONG all Odysseus' adventures, his brief stay among the Phæacians is generally accepted as the most interesting. Even more than the other marvels of the poem this is felt to be the happy invention of a great creative artist. And yet, like all the truly original figures of imaginative literature, Nausicaa is absolutely human and full of life. If there is any allegorical or moral significance in her story, or in this Scherian episode generally, it has remained happily undiscovered. There is no need of apology for devoting a section of our work to this immortal child of the poetic imagination, who is the happiest possible illustration both of the Humanity and of the Art of Homer.

For seven years the loveliest and gentlest of divinities, Calypso, the Lady of the Mist, has detained Odysseus in her fair wave-encircled isle, desiring him to be her husband. Yet, though all his companions have perished amid the miseries and dangers of the former voyages, he still pines, day and night, to venture forth once more, to brave the deadliest hate of the sea's lord, Poseidon, if perchance he may come, before he dies, home again to rugged, ungrateful Ithaca, to the faithful, prudent Penelope, who is, he well knows, no longer fair or young, and who could never have been a rival of Calypso's divine loveliness.

At last the heavenly gods have pity on the homesick exile, and Zeus orders Hermes to go to Calypso's island abode and bid her release Odysseus.

Let us hear Zeus' command to Hermes :—

"Hermes, since thou art also on other occasion our herald,
Tell to the nymph of the braided tresses our counsel unerring,
Even the homeward return of the patient-hearted Odysseus.
How he shall go, unaccompanied either of gods or of mortals :

Yet on a well-bound raft, though suffering
   grievous disaster,
On the twentieth day to the fertile land of
   Phæacians,
Scheria, he shall come, to a people like the
   immortals.
They shall send him by ship to his native
   country belovèd,
Giving him store of bronze and gold and
   raiment in plenty,
More than ever Odysseus had won for him-
   self out of Ilios,
Though he had fared untroubled, securing
   his share of the booty.
So it is destined that he shall see his loved
   ones, returning   •
Unto his high-roofed hall and unto the land
   of his fathers."   (Od. V. 29–42.)

Donning his winged sandals and clasping
his magic wand, the messenger Hermes set
forth without a murmur upon his errand.
He darted earthward, traversed the wide
purple sea, and neared the far-off island : —

Journeyed until he was come where the
   nymph of the beautiful tresses
Lived in a spacious cave ; and within her
   dwelling he found her.

There on the hearth was a great fire blaz-
    ing, and far through the island
Floated the fragrance of well-cleft cedar
    and sandal-wood burning.
She was herself within, with sweet voice
    singing, and meanwhile
Busy was she at the loom, and with golden
    shuttle was weaving.
Round and about her cave a luxuriant forest
    extended;
Poplar-trees were there, and alders, and
    odorous cypress.
. . . Four springs set in order with shining
    water were running:
Near were they to each other, yet turned in
    as many. directions.

(These four springs become, in the learnèd
argument of Dr. Warren already mentioned,
the four rivers of Eden.)

All about soft meadows of violets bloomed,
    and of parsley.
Even a deathless god might therefore, hither
    approaching,
Gaze upon what he saw, and be in spirit de-
    lighted.   (*Ibid.* 57–74.)

As the poet's last words plainly intimate,
such a trim, orderly scene was in truth the

Greek ideal of natural beauty, rather than a wider, more varied panorama, with snow-capped mountains for its frame. Perhaps the struggle of man with the savage forces of Nature was still too near and well remembered for him to find delight in her wilder aspects.

Homer assures us that the immortals always know each other when they meet, no matter how widely sundered their abodes; but not even in this enchanted spot do they have the power of reading each other's thoughts without words. Hermes, therefore, utters the bidding of Zeus, though in gentler and less imperative form, with a frank confession of his own unwillingness to bring the message. The poet then continues : —

So did he speak, and Calypso, divine
    among goddesses. shuddered.
Then she uttered to him these wingèd words,
    and made answer :
" Merciless are ye, O gods, and more than
    the rest are ye jealous,
Ye who, when goddesses openly mate with
    men, are indignant." (*Ibid.* 116–120.)

Calypso relates briefly how she rescued Odysseus when the wind and the billow drove him toward her isle, clinging to the keel of his wrecked vessel after all his comrades had perished. Such passing allusions to the hero's previous adventures are intended by the poet to arouse, rather than to gratify, the curiosity of his hearers. Odysseus, after his safe arrival at the court of the Phæacians, will relate his fortunes since the fall of Troy, just as Æneas, at Dido's banquet, tells the tale of his life. Calypso continues :—

"Often I said I would make him immortal
    and youthful forever.
Yet, for the purpose of Zeus, who is lord of
    the ægis, may nowise
Be by another divinity thwarted or kept
    from fulfilment,
Let him depart, since He hath so com-
    manded and bidden,
Over the restless sea. Nor yet myself will
    I send him,
Since no vessels equipped with oars are
    mine, nor companions,
Who on his way might bear him across the
    sea's broad ridges.

Yet will I heartily aid him with counsel,
    and hide from him nothing,
So that he all unscathed may come to the
    land of his fathers.''
(Ibid. 135–144.)

This prompt and sincere submission to the inevitable parting should win our sympathy the more fully for the gentle, loving nymph, who has nothing in common with capricious and cruel Circe. As Hermes hastens back to Olympos, Calypso seeks Odysseus in his favourite seat by the shore, and bids him no longer wear out his life with weeping, but straightway built a raft for his homeward voyage.

So did she speak, but the godlike, endur-
    ing Odysseus shuddered.
Then he uttered to her these wingèd words,
    and responded :
'' Surely some other intent, not merely
    to aid my departure,
Hast thou, in bidding me cross on a raft
    yon gulf of the waters,
Difficult, dread, that not even the well-
    shaped vessels may traverse,
Though so swiftly they fare, in the Zeus-
    sent breezes exultant.

Not on a raft would I set foot while thou
    art unwilling,
If thou consent not to swear with a mighty
    oath that in no wise
Thou wilt plot for me another and grievous
    disaster."   (*Ibid.* 171–179.)

Calypso, smiling and caressing him,
assures him of her good faith. She cannot, however, refrain from reminding him
of her own superiority in beauty to mortal women, and of the immortality which
she would have bestowed upon him. The
reply of Odysseus is perhaps more than
any other passage the keynote of the
poem : —

" Queen and goddess, for that, pray, be
    not wroth, for I also
Well am aware that the heedful Penelope,
    either in stature
Or in beauty of face, is, compared with
    thee, less noble.
She is a mortal, in truth, thou deathless and
    ageless forever.
Yet, even so, I all my days am wishful and
    eager
Homeward to make my way, and behold
    my day of returning.

If yet again some god on the wine-dark
    waters shall wreck me,
I will endure, with a heart in my breast
    that is patient of trouble.
Truly already I greatly have toiled and
    greatly have suffered,
Both on the waves and in war; and thereto let
    this also be added."   (*Ibid.* 215–224.)

The next four days are spent by Odysseus
in constructing the raft, which is elaborately
described, and deserves rather to be called
a boat. On the fifth day he sets sail, with
a goodly store of wine, water, and food,
provided by Calypso. For seventeen days
he voyages homeward, but on the eigh-
teenth Poseidon espies him from afar. The
sea-god's wrath is still hot on account of his
favourite son, the Cyclops Polyphemos, who
was blinded by Odysseus. A terrible storm
is aroused, the light craft is quickly stripped
of mast and sail, and Odysseus, still clinging to the wreck, is tossed about helpless
among the billows. But a semi-divine sea-
creature in feminine form comes to his aid.

Ino, of beautiful ankles, the daughter of
    Kadmos, beheld him, —

Leucothea, who once was of human speech
    and a mortal,
Now hath a share in the honours of gods in
    the depths of the waters.

The mortal Ino takes the name Leucothea
when transformed into a sea-divinity.   The
epithet " fair-ankled " is a favourite with
Homer, and is hardly introduced here to
assure us that Ino has not the form popu-
larly ascribed to a mermaid.

She took pity on exiled Odysseus in griev-
    ous misfortune.
Out of the watery deep she arose as rises a
    seagull,
Seated herself on the well-joined raft, and
    spoke, and addressed him :
  " Wretched one, why is Poseidon, the
    shaker of earth, thus embittered
Fiercely, so that he raises against thee full
    many disasters ?
Yet he shall not destroy thee, although so
    terribly wrathful.
Only do thou as I bid thee : thou seemest
    not lacking in shrewdness.
Strip off thy garments, and leave thy raft
    for the breezes to carry,
But do thou swim with thine arms, and
    struggle to win thee a landing

On the Phæacians' shore, whereon thou art
    destined to save thee.
Here, too, take this veil, and under thy
    breast shalt thou spread it, —
It is divine, — and have no fear that thou
    suffer or perish.
Yet, so soon as thou with thy hands shalt
    lay hold of the mainland,
Loosen it then from about thee, and into
    the wine-dark waters,
Ere thou turnest to go, thou shalt cast it
    afar from the sea-beach.''

(Ibid. 333–350.)

There is perhaps a reminiscence of this casting away of the magic veil in the tale of King Arthur's death, where Bedivere flings the sacred sword Excalibar back into the mere.

Odysseus hesitates, and is again fearful of treachery, as he was with Calypso. It may be that this constant dread of bad faith is the fitting penalty for his own excessive cunning and trickiness. But when a mighty billow utterly shatters his wrecked craft, and leaves him clinging to a single plank, the aid of the goddess is accepted. Poseidon now, with an exultant jeer, turns away, as he knows that Odysseus is not destined to perish on the sea; and Athene is permitted to quiet the waves and adverse winds. For two days and two nights the hero swims wearily onward, in constant fear of death. On the third morning, uplifted on a great wave, he sees the coast of Phæacia near at hand. But here a new peril awaits him. Once the mighty breaker dashes him against the steep cliffs that line the shore, but, carried back by the refluent wave, he has just strength to escape again outside the line of surf. Here he swims on parallel with the shore-line, until he feels the warmer current of a river which flows into the sea. To the river-god he straightway utters a fervent prayer.

"Hearken, O lord, whosoever thou art!
    unto thee, the much longed for,
Now am I come, in my flight from the sea
    and the threats of Poseidon.
Reverend even among the gods whose life
    is eternal
He is held, who comes as a wanderer, even
    as I now,
After my weary toil, am come to thy knees
    and thy current.

Show thou pity, O lord; for truly thy sup-
    pliant am I."   (*Ibid.* 445–450.)

Such passages as this make it clear that to
the Homeric poets the river-god was quite
as real as the stream itself. Perhaps not
one even among the Greeks of later ages,
save Æschylos in the Prometheus, is so
fully possessed by a belief in this conscious
personal life in forest, mountain, and stream.
There is far greater power of imagination,
and many-fold more poetic ingenuity, exerted
in shaping such a conception as the Sabrina
of Milton's Comus; but we are so much the
more aware of the poet's untiring efforts to
convince himself and us. The singer of the
Odyssey has no need to " make believe."

The river-god at once stays his stream,
and enables the weary swimmer to reach
the bank. Here, after a moment of utter
exhaustion, Odysseus casts the veil sea-
ward, and Leucothea's hands receive it:
the "lovely hands" which lingered in Milton's memory, and so are immortalized a
second time in a famous passage of Comus.
After some hesitation between the chilling

winds of the shore and the wild beasts of
the forest, he climbs the slope to the edge
of the wood, and lies down in the olive
thicket, covering himself with the dead
leaves.

And Athene

Over his eyes poured slumber, that she might
      straightway release him
From the fatigue of his grievous toil, by
      closing his eyelids.   (*Ibid.* 491–493.)

Such are the final words in the fifth book
of the Odyssey. Sometimes these Alexandrian divisions seem most mechanical and
inartistic : but the scenes of this book, at
any rate, have a natural connection and
unity, as well as a charm and beauty of
detail, which are of course lost in the mere
summary given here.

The scene now changes to the palace of
the Phæacian king, from which is to come
the aid so sorely needed by the shipwrecked
exile. The sixth book opens with the following lines :—

So did he slumber there, the enduring,
      godlike Odysseus,

Since he was overborne by fatigue and
    sleep; but Athene
Went meanwhile to the city and people of
    the Phæacians.
These had formerly dwelt within wide-
    wayed Hypereia,
Near to the Cyclops, a race of men exceed-
    ingly haughty,
Who had harassed them ever, and who were
    in force more mighty.
Then Nausithoös, like to a god, transplanted
    and led them
Unto Scheria, far removed from the traffick-
    ing nations.
Round their town he constructed a wall,
    and built habitations;
Temples, too, for the gods, and divided
    among them the cornlands.
Stricken by fate, he already had passed to
    the dwelling of Hades;
Now Alkinoös ruled; by the gods was he
    gifted with wisdom.
Toward his palace proceeded the gray-eyed
    goddess Athene,
Planning a homeward return for Odysseus,
    lofty of spirit.   (Od. VI. 1–14.)

This brief historical sketch of the Phæacians need give us no fear lest Odysseus, in

his eighteen days' voyage from Calypso's
island, may have crossed the boundary line
from fairyland into prosaic reality.   Hypereia, their former home, is merely "Upland,"
a casual invention of the poet.   Nausithoös,
their earlier leader, is simply "He of the
fleet ship"; and, indeed, nearly all the
names we meet in these Phæacian scenes
are derivatives from the Greek word $ναῦς$,
a ship.   The whole episode in Scheria is,
apparently, a rather sportive creation of
the Homeric fancy.   The allusion to the
Cyclops as their former neighbours is, no
doubt, intended to remind us that we are
not yet escaped from the realm of the
marvellous.

The latter half of the Odyssey is of a
quite different character, consisting almost
wholly of realistic scenes in Ithaca.   The
all-night homeward voyage of the sleeping
Odysseus on the magic bark of the Phæacians, at the beginning of the thirteenth
book, is the voyage from dreamland into
real life, and so the turning-point of the
entire story.

It will be seen that the writer declines to

accept the identification of Corcyra, the modern Corfu, with Scheria. In this scepticism he is emboldened by the protecting shield of the Ajax among English-speaking Hellenists. See Jebb's Introduction to Homer, page 46.

It is at the threshold of the episode in Scheria that we meet the lovable little princess Nausicaa, who is our proper subject. The frame of romance from which she steps forth to greet us enables us to enjoy the more fully the simplicity, the truthfulness to nature, and the idealized beauty of this slight but imperishable sketch. Let us venture to peep discreetly over Pallas Athene's august shoulder, as she enters her favourite's bower.

> Into a chamber most cunningly built she
> passed, where a maiden
> Sleeping lay, who in figure and face the immortals resembled,
> Named Nausicaa, child to Alkinoös, lofty of
> spirit.
> Maidens twain were beside her, with beauty
> endowed by the Graces;
> Near to the door they lay, and shut were the
> glimmering portals.

P

Fleet as the breath of the wind to the couch
of the maiden she darted.

(Ibid. 15–20.)

Athene assumes the guise of Nausicaa's
favourite girl companion as she speaks.

" Why did thy mother, Nausicaa, bear
thee a maiden so heedless ?
Shining raiment is thine, which now neg-
lected is lying ;
Yet is thy marriage at hand, when thou
must be fairly apparelled,
And must garments give unto those who
homeward shall lead thee,
Since thereby among men goes forth thy
good reputation.
Therein, too, is thy father delighted, and
reverend mother.
Come, with the dawning of day let us hasten
forth to the washing,
Seeing by no means long mayst thou yet
tarry a virgin.
Thou already art wooed by the noblest of
all the Phæacians
Everywhere, of the land wherein thou also
art native.
Come, now, urge at the dawning of day thy
illustrious father

Mules and a cart to make ready for thee, wherein thou wilt carry
Raiment of men, and robes, and the shining coverlets also.''
She, thus speaking, departed, the gray-eyed goddess Athene,
Unto Olympos, where we are told that the gods' habitation
Ever untroubled abides, nor yet by the tempests is shaken;
Nor is it wet by the rain, nor reached by snow, but about it
Clear is the cloudless air, and white is the sunshine upon it.
Through all ages within it the blessèd gods are rejoicing.
Having admonished the maid, the keen-eyed One thither departed.   (*Ibid.* 25–47.)

Among many imitations of this passage, the most familiar to us is, no doubt, the description of the "island valley of Avilion," to which Arthur hopes to pass, and where he may heal him of his grievous wound.

Presently morning came, enthroned in beauty, arousing
Graceful-robed Nausicaa: first at the vision she marvelled,

Then through her home she passed to repeat
    her dream to her parents,
Well-loved father and mother. She found
    them within, for the mother
Sat at the side of the hearth, in the midst of
    her women attendants,
Spinning the sea-dyed purple yarn; at the
    doorway her father
Met her, upon his way to join the illustrious
    chieftains,
Sitting in council, whither the noble Phæa-
    cians had called him.
Standing close at his side, she addressed
    her father belovèd: (*Ibid.* 48–56.)

(A more exact rendering for the next
words would be: "Papa, dear"; the term
of endearment being identical in Greek and
English, as in many other languages. Professor Merriam, in his excellent edition of
this portion of the Odyssey, The Phæacians
of Homer, quotes Pope's rendering of this
line, as a striking example of that translator's method in dealing with his original: —

"Will my dread sire his ear regardful deign,
And may his child the royal car obtain?")

"Father, dear, would you make ready for
    me a wagon, a high one,

Strong in the wheels, that I may carry our
    beautiful garments,
Those which now are lying soiled, to be
    washed in the river ?
Ay, and for you yourself it is seemly, when
    in the council
You with the chiefs are sitting, to have fresh
    raiment upon you.
Five dear sons besides within your palace
    are living ;
Two of them married already, but three yet
    blooming and youthful.''

(Ibid. 57–63.)

The keen observation in the next line
is evidently applicable more especially to
the three blooming young bachelor brothers
of the wilful little maid : —

" They are desirous always of having the
    new-washed garments
When to the dance they go. Of all this in
    my mind am I thoughtful.''
Thus did she speak, for she shamed her
    fruitful marriage to mention.

(Ibid. 64–66.)

This omission is, however, by no means
the only variation between the words of
Pallas and those of Nausicaa. The girl's

quick wit and ingenuity are abundantly
indicated in this seemingly artless speech.
Her innocent craft in leaving her chief
motive unuttered does not trouble her indulgent parent.

Yet understanding all this her affectionate
    father made answer:
"Neither the mules, my daughter, nor any-
    thing else do I grudge thee."
                        (*Ibid.* 67–68.)

So, in obedience to the king's command,
the mule-team is at once harnessed in the
courtyard of the palace.

Meantime, the maiden brought from the
    chamber the shining garments.
These on the polished wagon she carefully
    placed, and the mother
Put in a basket food of all kinds, suiting her
    wishes.
Dainties as well she packed, and into a
    bottle of goat-skin
Poured some wine; and the maiden had
    meanwhile mounted the wagon.
Liquid olive-oil in a golden vial she gave
    her,
After the bath to anoint herself and the
    women attendants.

Into her hands then the whip and the reins
    all shining she gathered,
Scourged them to run, and loud was the
    sound of the clattering mule-hoofs.
They unceasingly hastened, and carried the
    maid with the garments ;
Yet not alone, but with her there followed
    the women attendants. (*Ibid.* 74-84.)

Though the goddess Athene has inter-
fered in person to control the action of the
princess, yet the train of events just described is so naturally and vividly drawn
out, the meeting which is evidently to be
brought about is being prepared so easily
and credibly, that we ourselves seem to be
glancing in eager expectation from the exhausted hero, asleep in the thicket, to the
bright-eyed charioteer, followed by her
troop of merry companions, as she approaches the river-mouth.

When they now had arrived at the beautiful
    stream of the river,—
Where were the pools unfailing, and clear
    and abundant the water
Gushed from beneath, sufficient for cleans-
    ing the foulest of raiment, —

There did the girls unharness the mules
  from under the wagon.
Then they drove them to graze by the side
  of the eddying river,
Cropping the fragrant clover. But they
  themselves from the wagon
Took in their arms the garments, and carried
  them into the water,
Trod them there in the pits, — commencing
  a rivalry straightway.

(What could be more realistic than this
girlish determination to make a frolic even
of the most wearisome drudgery ?)

Then, when they had washed and cleansed
  completely the garments,
Spread them in order along by the beach of
  the sea, where the billow,
Dashing against the shore most strongly,
  was washing the pebbles.
When they had bathed and anointed themselves with the oil of the olive,
Then by the bank of the river the noonday
  meal they provided,
Waiting until their clothes should dry in
  the glow of the sunshine.
Presently, when they were sated with eat-
  ing, the maids and the princess

Started a game of ball, first laying aside
    their head-dress.   (*Ibid.* 85–100.)

The elaborate comparison of Nausicaa to
Artemis, which follows, will be most familiar to many readers through the close
imitation, or rather translation, of it by
Virgil, who applies it, with less fitness, to
Dido.

Foremost in song and in dance white-armed
    Nausicaa led them,
Even as Artemis passes, the huntress, over
    the mountains,
She who in chasing the boar or the fleet
    deer taketh her pastime;
With her the nymphs, the daughters of
    Zeus, who is lord of the ægis,
Woodland-dwellers, are sporting; and Leto
    rejoices in spirit;
Loftily over them all her head and brow she
    upraises.
All are beautiful there, yet she is easily
    foremost.
So in the midst of her girls was supreme
    that maiden unwedded.
              (*Ibid.* 101–109.)

The poet now again mentions Pallas,
and describes her as intervening once more

at this point to control the course of events
in Odysseus' interest.   This passing reminder of the *deus ex machina* does not,
however, prevent the simple idyllic plot
from unravelling itself in a most natural
and unforced manner.

Then did the princess throw their ball at
  one of the handmaids.
Yet she missed the girl, and it fell in the
  eddying river.
So they screamed full loudly : — and godlike Odysseus was wakened,
Sat upright, and pondered within his heart
  and his spirit :
 " Woe is me !   What mortals are these
  whose land I have entered ?
Are they lawless, I wonder, and savage, re-
  gardless of justice ?
Or are they kind unto strangers, and rev'rent
  the spirit within them ?
Surely a womanish cry, as of maidens, re-
  sounded about me.
Nymphs, it may be, that dwell on the
  cragged peaks of the mountains,
Or that live in the sources of rivers and
  grassy morasses.
Or am I near, perchance, unto human language and mortals ?

Come, now, let me myself make trial there-
of, and behold them."
Having thus spoken, the godlike Odysseus
crept from the bushes;
Yet with his powerful hand he broke off a
branch in the thicket,
Covered with foliage, to hide his nakedness,
screening his body. (*Ibid.* 115–129.)

The comparison of Odysseus to a hun-
gry lion leaving his covert, which occurs
here, may be omitted; its chief value
being to illustrate the indebtedness of the
poet who composed the Odyssey to the
older Iliad. The figure is much more
effective, as originally employed, in describing Sarpedon rushing eagerly to battle.

Loathsome to them he appeared, by the
brine of the sea disfigured.
Hither and thither they fled to the jutting
points of the shoreland.
Only Alkinoös' daughter remained; for
Athene imparted
Courage into her heart, and conquered the
terror within her. (*Ibid.* 137–140.)

Under the circumstances, Odysseus did
not venture to approach and clasp the

princess' knees, — the regular attitude for
a suppliant to assume, — but, standing
aloof from her, he

Straightway uttered to her a speech that was
      winning and crafty, —   (*Ibid.* 148.)

an art in which he was above all men a
master.

    "I am thy suppliant, princess! Art thou
       some god or a mortal?
If thou art one of the gods that have their
       abode in the heavens,
Unto Artemis, child of imperial Zeus, do I
       deem thee
Likest in beauty of face, as well as in stature
       and bearing.
But if of mortals thou'rt one, that have on
       the earth their abiding,
Trebly blessèd in thee are thy father and
       reverend mother,
Trebly blessèd thy brethren; and surely the
       spirit within them
Glows evermore with delight for thy sake
       when they behold thee
Entering into the dance, who art so lovely
       a blossom.
Happy in heart is he, moreover, above all
       others,

Who by gifts shall prevail, and unto his
    dwelling shall lead thee.
Never before with mine eyes have I beheld
    such a mortal,
Whether a woman or man.   As I gaze, awe
    seizes upon me ! ''   (*Ibid.* 149–161.)

Casting about in his mind for a comparison, he can only liken her to a graceful young palm-tree which he had once seen at Delos, beside Apollo's altar. The passage is of interest for two quite distinct reasons. It shows that in the poet's day, at any rate, the island-sanctuary of Apollo was already noted, and visited by voyagers from other Greek lands; and also that the palm-tree was then a rare and much-admired novelty in the Ægean. With a brief reference to his latest voyage, in which it may be noted that he makes no allusion to the gracious creatures of her own sex who had cherished or aided him, he continues : —

" Yet have mercy, O queen ! After suffer-
    ing many disasters,
First unto thee am I come. I know not one
    of the others
Whoso make their home within this city or
    country.

But do thou show me the town, and give me
    some tattered garment,
If perchance when thou camest some wrap
    thou hadst for the linen."

(Ibid. 175–179.)

But close upon this most humble request
and almost extravagant self-abasement, the
unknown wanderer ends his appeal with
noble and pathetic words.

" So may the gods accord thee whatever in
    spirit thou cravest :
Husband and home may they grant, and
    glorious harmony also.
Since there is nothing, in truth, more mighty
    than this, or more noble,
When two dwell in a home concordant in
    spirit together,
Husband and wife : unto foes a source of
    many vexations,
Joy to their friends ; yet they themselves
    most truly shall know it ! "

(Ibid. 180–185.)

Either the compliments at the beginning
of this speech, or the tender sentiments at
the close, have already produced a powerful
effect upon the heart of the gentle princess.

Then unto him in her turn white-armed
    Nausicaa answered :
" Stranger, thou dost not seem an ignoble
    man, nor a senseless ;
Zeus, the Olympian, himself apportions their
    blessings to mortals,
Both to the base and the noble, to each as
    suiteth his pleasure ;
This hath he laid upon thee, and thou must
    in patience endure it.
Yet now, since thou into our state art
    entered, and country,
Neither of raiment shalt thou be in lack,
    nor of aught whatsoever
Is for a hard-pressed suppliant, meeting
    with succour, befitting.
Yes, and the town I will show thee, and tell
    thee the name of the people.
'Tis the Phæacians who dwell in this our
    city and country.
I myself am the child of Alkinoös, lofty of
    spirit,
On whom all the Phæacians' dominion and
    force are dependent."

(Then turning aside from him, the princess
recalls the fugitive maidens.)

" Stay, my attendants ! Why at behold-
    ing a man are ye fleeing ?

Did ye suppose him, perchance, to be of a
    hostile nation ?
Surely no man is alive, nor shall he be liv-
    ing hereafter,
Who would venture to enter the land of the
    men of Phæacia
Offering harm ; for we of the gods are dearly
    belovèd.
Out of the way, too, we dwell, in the midst
    of the billowy waters,
Farthest of all mankind ; no others have
    dealings among us.
Nay, this is some ill-fated man come wan-
    dering hither,
Whom we must care for now, because all
    strangers and beggars
Stand in the charge of Zeus, and a gift,
    though little, is welcome.
Come, then, give both drink and food to
    the stranger, and bid him
Bathe in the stream, my attendants, where
    from the wind there is shelter.''

(Ibid. 186–210.)

Odysseus is accordingly provided with
robe and tunic and the vial of olive-oil.
After he has bathed and anointed himself,
Pallas Athene makes him far statelier and
more beautiful than before. So, as he sits

resting a little apart, Nausicaa addresses her companions with truly Homeric frankness.

> "Listen to me, my white-armed maids, that I something may tell you.
> Not without the approval of all the gods in Olympos
> Hath this man come hither, among the Phæacians, the godlike.
> 'Tis but a brief while since that I really thought him uncomely.
> Now is he like to the gods who abide in the open heavens.
> Would that such an one as he could be called my husband,
> Having his dwelling here and contented among us to tarry!"
>
> (*Ibid.* 239–245.)

It will be interesting to set here, for comparison, a few lines from the greatest of our contemporary English poets, who long ago, introducing his earliest Arthurian verses as

> "Weak Homeric echoes, nothing worth,"

intimated thereby his own consciousness of a kinship in spirit which many of his readers have recognized.

Q

"Marr'd as he was, he seem'd the goodliest
    man
That ever among ladies ate in hall,
And noblest, when she lifted up her eyes.
However marr'd, of more than twice her
    years,
Seam'd with an ancient sword-cut on his
    cheek,
And bruised and bronzed, she lifted up her
    eyes
And loved him, with that love that was her
    doom."

Nausicaa again orders that food and drink
be set before the stranger, and the poet records that he ate ravenously ; adding apolo-
getically that he

    long from food had been fasting.

A vigorous appetite is a constant characteristic of Odysseus in the Iliad and Odyssey.
On one occasion, in the former tale, he is
employed on arduous enterprises nearly all
night ; and a careful reader, if not absorbed
in the loftier features of the poem, may note
that thrice between sunset and morning he
accepts an invitation to a hearty meal, and
apparently on each occasion does full jus-

tice to the cheer. This thoroughly human trait has not escaped the attention of the poet who invented this Phæacian episode, and who certainly was in little danger of erring in the direction of excessive dignity and seriousness. When Odysseus, despite this breaking of his fast, makes a pathetic appeal for food to Nausicaa's parents, a few hours later, it is in words whose extravagance is carried to the verge of grotesqueness. Among the heroes of the mythic age, perhaps Heracles only is more notable as a valiant trencher-knight.

Nausicaa now makes preparations for her return homeward, and, having mounted the wagon, she thus addresses Odysseus: —

"Stranger, arise, and townward fare, that
      I may conduct thee
Unto the house of my wise father, in which
      I assure thee
Thou shalt behold whosoever are noblest of
      all the Phæacians.
Yet thou must do as I say: thou seem'st
      not lacking in shrewdness.
While we are passing along by the fields and
      the farms of our people,

So far among my maids, close after the
    mules and the wagon
Thou mayst come, with speed, and I will
    be guide on the journey.
But as we come to the town, round which
    is a high-built rampart,
And upon either side of the city a beautiful
    harbour " —   (*Ibid.* 255–263.)

Nausicaa runs off into an admiring description of her home, until she is even
guilty of forgetting the main clause of her
original sentence !   It appears that the narrow road over the isthmus into the town is
the favourite resort of idlers, whose discour-
teous remarks the princess dreads to face
in Odysseus' company.   With quick fancy
she imagines what they would say : —

" ' Who is yon stranger who follows Nau-
    sicaa ?   Handsome and stately
Is he.   Where did she find him ?   She'll
    have him herself for her husband !
Either she rescued him as a castaway out
    of his vessel,
One of a far-off people, — since none there
    are who are near us, —
Or some god much prayed for is down from
    the heavens descended

> At her petition, and he for his wife shall
>   have her forever.
> So is it better, if she has gone and found
>   her a husband
> Out of another land, for these of her folk,
>   the Phæacians,
> She disdains, though many and excellent men
>   are her suitors.' "   (*Ibid.* 276–284.)

Lest we should fancy the last words to be a mere fiction of Nausicaa to raise herself in the handsome stranger's esteem, the poet has taken care to put the same assertion, in somewhat stronger form, into the mouth of Pallas Athene, when she appears in the night to the princess, at the opening of the sixth book.

> " So would they talk, and for me it would
>   be a disgrace ! — and I also
> Should with another girl be angry, whoever
>   so acted ;
> Who, in spite of her friends, while her father
>   and mother were living,
> Mingled freely with men, ere yet she was
>   publicly wedded."   (*Ibid.* 285–288.)

It is quite possible that these very proper remarks of the king's daughter, on the duty

of maidenly modesty, are prompted in part by
the consciousness that her own innocent lo-
quacity has just carried her somewhat too far.

> "Stranger, and thou must now to my
>   words give attention, that quickly
> Thou mayst obtain safe-conduct, and home-
>   ward return, from my father.
> Near to the road thou wilt notice a beautiful
>   grove of Athene, —
> Poplars: within it a fountain flows, and a
>   meadow surrounds it.
> There my father's domain is found, and his
>   fruitful enclosure."   (*Ibid.* 289–293.)

Here, then, outside the town, Odysseus is
to remain behind until the girls have had
time to reach home. Then he also may
pass into the city, where he will have no
difficulty in finding the palace, so inferior
are the ordinary Phæacian houses to the
stately abode of Alkinoös.

> " But so soon as the hero's dwelling and
>   courtyard receive thee
> Make thy way at once through the hall, till
>   thou come to my mother.
> She has her seat at the side of the hearth,
>   in the gleam of the firelight,

Spinning her yarn, sea-purple in colour, a
    marvel to look on, —
Leaning on one of the columns. Her hand-
    maids are seated behind her."
                (*Ibid.* 303–307.

The unwearied diligence of Arete, the
queen, whom Odysseus will find at dusk
employed as her daughter had left her in
the early morning, may well remind us of
Priscilla, the Puritan maiden, and Bertha,
the beautiful spinner.

"On that selfsame pillar my father's chair
    is resting.
There he sits, and like an immortal his wine
    he is quaffing.
Yet thou must pass him by, and unto the
    knees of my mother
Stretch thy hands, that thou mayst behold
    thy day of returning
Quickly and joyfully, though thy land is
    exceedingly distant." (*Ibid.* 308–312.)

The keen-witted little princess has already
discovered who is the real ruler in cabin
and hall.

The sun is setting when they reach the
sacred grove of Pallas, where Odysseus

obediently tarries behind, and makes a fervent prayer to the goddess of the sanctuary. Here the sixth book closes.

From the seventh book, which describes the reception of Odysseus in the palace, we can cull only a few of the opening lines.

> There did he make his prayer, the god-
>   like, enduring Odysseus,
> While on her way to the city the strong
>   mules carried the maiden.
> When she now had arrived at her father's
>   glorious palace,
> There at the doorway she checked them.
>   Around her were gathered her
>   brothers,
> — Like unto gods were they to behold, —
>   and they from the wagon
> Straightway unharnessed the mules, and
>   carried the raiment within doors.
> She to her chamber passed, where an ancient
>   dame from Apeira
> Lighted a fire for her, — her servant Eury-
>   medousa ;
> . . . Lighted a fire in her room, and there
>   made ready her supper.
>   (Od. VII. 1–13.)

So Nausicaa slips quietly out of the story.
Only once more do we have a glimpse of
her. Odysseus meets with the kindly reception which she had promised him. All
the next day he is entertained with athletic
contests, dancing, and the harper's lay.
The story of this day fills the eighth book.
At nightfall, after a luxurious bath, he is
descending to the banquet-hall.

But Nausicaa, who by the gods was gifted
    with beauty,
There in the well-built hall at the side of a
    pillar was standing.
On Odysseus gazed she with wonder when
    she beheld him ;
Then these wingèd words she uttered to him
    and addressed him :
" Farewell, stranger ! And in thy native
    country hereafter
Think of me, unto whom thou first for thy
    life art indebted."
Thus did the crafty Odysseus address her
    then and responded :
" O Nausicaa, noble-hearted Alkinoös'
    daughter,
Verily so may Zeus, the Thunderer, hus-
    band of Herè,

Grant that I come to my home, and behold
    my day of returning, .
As, even there, unto thee as a god I would
    pay my devotions,
All my days, evermore ; for my life thou
    hast rescued, O maiden.''
             (Od. VIII. 457–468.)

The epithet '' crafty '' is the usual one of
Odysseus, and need have no reference to
the situation at the moment. But surely
it *is* a proof of consummate skill, as well as
of the highest courtesy, when he thus, with
magnificent hyperbole, in his hasty words
of final farewell, elevates to the position of
a goddess, or of a patron saint as it were,
the pure-hearted girl who had so frankly
intimated her desire to retain him in a
closer relation.   What other parting words
could have done so much to heal the hurt
and save her pride ? Tennyson could de-
vise none, but must needs let even courtly
Lancelot ride sadly away without farewell.

'' This was the one discourtesy that he used.''

And so Odysseus and Nausicaa part ; for
not even in merry Phæacia does the Greek

poet venture to let a young girl mingle with the men in the banquet-hall.

Of the hero's later fortunes all the world knows. At the banquet, the minstrel, singing of the siege of Troy, stirs the unknown guest to tears, and, being courteously questioned by his host, Odysseus reveals his name, the most illustrious of all who survived the fatal strife in the Scamandrian plain. The next four books of the poem, from the ninth to the twelfth, contain his account of former wanderings on the homeward voyage from the Troad. After another day spent in feasting and in listening to the harper Demodocos, he is permitted at nightfall to embark for home. He straightway falls into a deep sleep, and is still slumbering heavily when the Phæacians set him ashore, with many precious gifts, upon a remote corner of his own rugged Ithaca.

The last twelve books of the poem relate how, by craft and valour, he won his throne and wife again. Later poets, of every age and speech, have attempted to weave still farther the web of his adventurous life. In one of the most beautiful cantos of the

Inferno, he himself tells the tale of his last voyage and death, and Tennyson's poem Ulysses is so perfect in form and so touching in thought as to make us willingly forget, with the poet, that Odysseus' faithful comrades,

> " Who ever with a frolic welcome took
> The storm and sunshine,"

had all perished on the way, before the hero came again to his own.

But of Nausicaa the Odyssey has not another word to tell ; and what later singer might venture to bid her live even a single day more ?

> " Ah, who shall lift that wand of magic power,
> Or the lost clue regain ? "

One Attic drama may indeed have included among its characters a Nausicaa, drawn by a not unworthy hand. We are told that when Sophocles' play Nausicaa, or the Washers, was acted, the poet broke through his usual custom and himself appeared as an actor, winning much applause, especially by his beauty and grace in the

dancing and rhythmic ball-play, in the
character of Nausicaa herself! This incident has been curiously overlooked by Mr.
Browning in a passage of his learnèd Aris-
tophanes' Apology : —

. . . " Once, and only once, trod stage,
Sang, and touched lyre in person, in his youth
Our Sophokles."

It has been intimated more than once
already that the translator sees, or fancies
he sees, a striking, though purely accidental,
resemblance between the stories of Nausicaa
and of the lily maid of Astolat.   Each loves
at first sight the most illustrious hero of her
day, when he comes, unknown and unaccompanied, to her home.   Each saves the life
of the stranger, and proffers him a pure
maidenly love which he cannot return.
Even the circumstances of the good knight's
final departure are not wholly unlike in the
two tales ; for when Odysseus, embarking
for home, bids a grateful and loving farewell to his hosts, he does not venture to
mention Nausicaa by name, and it is not
certain that she was present.   The wan-

derer's last words are addressed to Arete, the queen, invoking a blessing on her household and her folk.

And yet, surely no one would be tempted to press the parallel farther, and to fancy that the Phæacian mind pined away, like Elaine, for love of her lost hero. When, at the banquet, the night before his depart- ure, the shipwrecked stranger revealed him- self as Odysseus, far famed above all men, the destroyer of Ilios, the exciting news doubtless spread through the servants' hall to the women's rooms, and faithful old Eurymedousa brought the tidings, per- chance, even to the sequestered chamber of the princess. Nausicaa's heart may have stirred with pride to think that so long as the strange story of the crafty Ith- acan's life should be told or sung, in after- days, she would always live in one of its brightest scenes ; but the husband of heed- ful Penelope, the father of Telemachos, must quickly have lost the power over her heart which the unknown suppliant had so easily gained. If Telemachos' wanderings had brought *him* to that sunny Scherian beach — But let us cast no tempting suggestion in the path of any too audacious nineteenth-century would-be Homerid ! Indeed, this same happy solution has already occurred to the mind of a later Hellenic poet.

And the moral ? It has been uttered already in memorable words. There was a learned but inconclusive discussion in *The New York Nation*, I believe, some years ago, whether it was a pagan sage or a Christian saint who coined the aphorism, "*Maledicti qui ante nos nostra dixerunt.*" (Confusion to those who have said our good things before us.) It matters little, however, which invented the phrase, for the sentiment is one of which the church father or the heathen philosopher alike should have been ashamed. What has really never been said had better not be said, because it is presumably false ; and we never lose the privilege of trying to utter the old thought better than all others have done, and so making it our own. But, more than that, one of the greatest debts we owe to our predecessors is their simple, adequate utterance of great and inspiring truths, in such impressive form that they pass current like perfect and indestructible coin, making every generation of common men so much the richer by each philosophic maxim or golden poetic phrase.

And certainly, it was only with delight that the translator, just as he was undertaking the present sketch, welcomed a little lay sermon on the tale of Nausicaa (Simplicity, by Charles Dudley Warner, *Atlantic Monthly*, March, 1889), so brief and graceful, so full and suggestive, that it would be presumptuous indeed to add thereto, or even to attempt a summary of the essay in question. It may be permitted, however, to call attention to a single sentence in that paper: "I am not recalling it" (the story of Nausicaa) "because it is a conspicuous instance of the true realism that is touched with the ideality of genius, which is the immortal element in literature, but as an illustration of the other necessary quality in all productions of the human mind that remain age after age, and that is simplicity." It is to be hoped that we may yet have from the same hand that other lesson which is thus given only passing mention; for the essayist is evidently in agreement with us that Nausicaa is as happy an example as could well be found, not only of the essential simplicity of the greatest artistic creations, but of the other indispensable requirements, — truthfulness and beauty; or, as he apparently prefers to combine the two in one, truthfulness to the beautiful side of humanity or nature, which is infinitely more real and eternal than ugliness and imperfection.

The episode of Nausicaa was not written, like Bekker's Charicles, to illustrate the everyday life of the ancient Greeks. It cannot be used as evidence regarding, *e.g.* the frequency of washing-days in the Homeric age. It is no proof that Hellenic princesses went picnicking in remote spots, unprotected and unchaperoned. It is a romance. The whole Phæacian episode (every Homeric episode, indeed) is inextricably intertwined with marvellous and superhuman incidents and characters. But it is true, nevertheless, — true to the essen-

R

tial laws of art and of humanity. And therefore of Nausicaa, as of Rosalind, of Perdita, or of Miranda, it may well be asked, " Who, pray, is alive, if she be dead ? "

VII

THIS paper is intended to sketch out a concrete illustration of a familiar truth, or even perhaps of two truths. In order to remind ourselves that classical studies should be alive and progressive, not plodding a dull circle, nor rambling in dusty catacombs, it is helpful to remember that the antique world itself the object of our study, teems with multifarious warring life from whatever side we gaze upon it. We cannot enforce unity and permanence where infinite variation is itself a law. This is especially true of myth.

There is a passage at the end of Euripides' Hippolytos, in which Artemis calmly explains — while the poor hero himself lies a pain-racked victim to a celestial quarrel

—the charming harmony that reigns on Olympos.

"Not one would interfere to thwart the will
Of any, but we ever stand aloof."

Makers of mythological handbooks, from Apollodoros' Bibliotheke to Murray's Manual, seem desirous to apply the precept of Artemis rather than to observe the practice of her family. They would bid us gaze upon a fairly-ordered garden, as it were, wherein every bed has but its own well-bred flowers, while the walks are broad and straight, never labyrinthine. But the truth —as a glance, even, into Pausanias' accumulation of local legends and contradictory cults would alone suffice to remind us — is rather to be seen in the figure of a tropical jungle. Livy makes a naïve attempt to open a fairly straight vista through this jungle, that we may see our way from the Pergamos of Troy to the hill town of Romulus. But his contemporary, Dionysios, who crowds into the first chapter of his Archaiologia the whole mass of Latin founders' legends, has given a much better

idea how myths look in their native luxu-
riance.

Even in the great overshadowing and per-
manently located legends, like the greatest
of all, the "tale of Troy divine," it is not
merely fanciful to suggest a resemblance
to the mangrove tree, whose farthest
branches take root in alien soil to become the sturdy trunks of an independent
growth. We cannot enforce symmetry in
that growth by any process short of killing
the tree and cutting it into boards. Infinitely more scientific is the attempt to
follow historically the story of development.

The other truth is perhaps best stated
in Cicero's familiar words : "*Omnes artes,
quæ ad humanitatem pertinent, habent
quoddam vinculum, et quasi cognatione
quadam inter se continentur.*" Fragmen-
tary and baffling enough our knowledge
will always remain ; but from every cam-
paign is borne home in triumph the sculptured sarcophagus or inscribed tablet,
carven gem or painted vase, destined to
throw new light on the old puzzles, — and

to evoke new problems no less. Indeed, the soil of classical lands sometimes seems to our excited imagination to be slowly producing and steadily multiplying these treasures, as the earth does her diamonds or the ocean his pearls. The second truism is, then, that every department of scientific study, whether referring to linguistics and literature or to the Realities (*Realien*), throws its ray of illustration on every other. After a popular lecture, the question was once asked why Andromache was regularly described as white-armed. Among a half-dozen evasions to conceal his own ignorance, the lecturer pleased the questioner best by the reminder, that it was the ordinary convention with the decorators of ancient pottery to represent the exposed flesh of women as white, not, like the men's, red: this being again a memorial of the harem-like seclusion in which most Greek ladies passed their lives.

A few of the main features in the modern or complete Troy-myth will perhaps best illustrate how constantly the Greek mind incrusted new details upon the old legends;

just as many a generation added new finials
and gargoyles, statues and ornaments of
every kind, to a Gothic cathedral, even
after it might be pronounced finished. A
Greek was hardly capable of mere slavish
copying; even the humble artisan who
painted earthen pottery hardly ever merely
borrowed a *motif* from epic story or the
more familiar scenes of tragedy.   He introduces, omits, recombines, according to his
fancy and the limits of his material.

That is just what Pindar or Sophocles
did, too, in a lordlier way. For instance,
Pindar, retelling the whole Pelops-myth,
after a new fashion, in the first Olympian,
says: "I cannot call one of the blessed
Gods a cannibal!"   Plutarch has been
called unscientific for proposing to omit
certain lines from Homer on purely sub-
jective and ethical grounds. Yet not only
a Pindar or a Plato shows sympathy with
such criticism. The great Aristarchos himself, prince of textual critics, it will be
recalled, struck out two lines from the Iliad
solely because they ascribed to Thetis a
sentiment unworthy of ideal motherhood.

If we should begin to tell to a child the
complete tale of Troy in systematic fashion,
as Apollodoros has done in meagre prose,
or Andrew Lang in his delightful poem,
Helen of Troy, we should start perhaps after
this fashion : " At Peleus' and Thetis' wedding the unbidden guest Eris cast among the
divinities an apple inscribed, $\tau\hat{\eta}$ $\kappa\alpha\lambda\lambda\acute{\iota}\sigma\tau\eta$"
(For the Fairest), etc. And, by the way,
this wedding of Thetis, with the presence
of the gods there, may serve as an instructive illustration of our two truisms.

Possibly our earliest authority for the
whole subject is — not a literary account at
all but — the famous François vase, which
plays also so large a part in the history
of ancient vase-painting and epigraphy.
Furthermore, the most vivid and poetical
summary of the various details is found in
Catullus' longest poem. Yet even within
these four hundred and eight lines are concealed startling combinations. For instance,
Peleus the Argonaut and Thetis the Nereid
first behold each other when that earliest
of vessels, created with magic powers under
Pallas' own guidance, first disturbs the

waters till then untraversed by ships. The youthful mariner, leaning over the rail, and the sea-nymph, rising to the surface with her inquisitive sisters, gaze into each other's eyes, and are fired with love at the first glance. Yet upon the coverlet of their bridal bed is embroidered the desertion of Ariadne by Theseus. That is, the gradual growth of the Greek marine, the rise of Cretan power, the conquest of Athens, and imposition of human tribute, the voyages and adventures of Theseus, lay between. The courtship of the impetuous Nereid must evidently have lasted, then, from two to three hundred years. Such are the difficulties of classic poet or modern scholar who attempts to weave mythic materials into any connected patchwork.

Thetis' wedding, we said, is the natural starting-point, now, for the Tale of Helen. But as a matter of fact the Judgment of Paris is mentioned only in two verses of Iliad, XXIV., a late book; and these verses, 29–30, are themselves an awkward interpolation.

> . . . Who did the goddesses anger when
>   they had entered his courtyard;
> Her he approved who indulged his fatal
>   wantonness for him.

The latter half of the preceding line, "Because of the madness of Paris," occurs repeatedly elsewhere in the Iliad, but referring always merely to Paris' sin in carrying off Helen. This is, in fact, as was said elsewhere, the first link in the chain of evils known to the poet of the Iliad. The later Cyprian Epic, written expressly to ascribe more adequate causes for the war, pieced on the famous introduction : and, still later, a rhapsode probably interpolated this awkward couplet into the Iliad, thus giving, ignorantly or wilfully, a perverse twist to verse 28.

Again, Hecabè's dream, the night before Paris' birth, that she bore, not a child, but a firebrand that set all Troy-town in flames, can hardly be traced to an earlier author than Euripides. The passage is in his Troades (919–922). Helen, accused by the queen-mother, is making one of those long clever retorts in which Euripides delights, and striving to lay the whole blame for the war upon poor old Hecabè herself, and upon Priam.

"*She* first produced the author of these woes,
In bearing Paris.   Next the aged king
Ruined me and Troy, when he slew not the babe,
The firebrand's hateful image, Alexandros."

Of course Euripides may not have been the first to invent this dream.   Indeed, he speaks of it here as of something familiarly known. But Homer would hardly have failed to touch upon it, if known to him, in the many bitter denunciations of Paris.   Euripides treated parts of the Trojan legend in more than half his extant plays, and in many others now known only from fragments. Undoubtedly he added many clever touches to the story.   This whole tale of Alexander's (or Paris') childhood, his exposure on Mount Ida, the life among the shepherds, his rediscovery and restoration to the royal palace, were treated by Euripides in a special play, Alexandros, of which little remains.

Homer, again, does not say the Greek princes were all Helen's suitors, and had bound themselves by oath to rescue her if taken from the husband of her choice (or of her father's choice). Thucydides (I. 9) saw that the story of the oath was incredible, and suggested that the heroes were really Agamemnon's vassals. This is clearly not true of the Homeric Achilles, who is free to go or to stay in Troy, and who says haughtily that he came merely to gratify the Atreidæ (Iliad, I. 152-160). The story of the oath in some form is, however, as old as Hesiod, who, in a lost work, gave a catalogue of Helen's suitors. This did not include Achilles (Pausanias, III. 24. 10). Euripides makes him one in his play, Helena (vs. 99). "He came as Helen's suitor, we have heard." No passage, however, even of Euripides, could carry less presumption of antiquity. Euripides in this play as a whole introduces the boldest of variations from the Trojan story even as told by himself in earlier dramas! In particular, Helen never goes to Troy at all, but is detained in Egypt, while the heroes slay each other in the Troad over a mere *eidolon* in her guise.

Whatever the force that gathered and holds together the great armament, the commander-in-chief, Menelaos' brother Agamemnon, is quite overshadowed by Achilles, the resistless son of Thetis the sea-nymph : but that she had been wooed by Zeus and other gods, and given instead to the mortal Peleus because destined to bear a son mightier than his father, is first stated by Pindar: (Isthmian, VIII. 30–44) unless we regard the appearance of Zeus and the other gods at a mortal's wedding, represented upon the François vase, as earlier testimony to the same effect.

The son, as he is himself aware, is destined to a long and peaceful, or to a brief and glorious existence (Iliad, IX. 410–416). There is a pretty story that his father therefore sent Achilles off to the island of Skyros, where he was dressed and educated as a girl among the king's daughters : a strange transition from the wild life among the Thessalian hills, where he speared lions as he galloped on the centaur Cheiron's back.

(The shifting scenes in Achilles' brief life
are very happily indicated upon a late relief in the form of a well-curb, which is in
the Capitoline Museum.) To Skyros, when
the band goes forth for the war, he is
tracked by Odysseus, who discovers his
identity by a shrewd device. Amid a bas-
ketful of jewels and trinkets offered to the
princesses, a gleaming sword is concealed.
When the fairest among the young girls —
for such the youthful figure seemed — approaches in turn to choose, the flash of the
brand catches the eye, and betrays the sex,
of Peleus' child. The scene where Achilles
is just drawing forth the shining blade is
represented in numerous works of art, ancient and modern. (Besides the "well-
curb" just mentioned, see especially the
fine Pompeian wall painting, which is out-
lined in Baumeister's Denkmäler des Clas-
sischen Alterthums, Plate L.)

This romantic story cannot be clearly
traced farther back than Sophocles' play,
The Skyrian Women, of which very little
is preserved. It seems clearly the invention of a more romantic age than Homer's,

perhaps devised to explain an allusion of the youthful Achilles (Iliad, XIX. 326) to a "dear son who is growing up in Skyros." The later legend makes Achilles the father of Neoptolemos, when himself hardly in his teens, by one of the Skyrian princesses, his playmates. But Leaf and other editors would expunge all allusions to Neoptolemos from the Iliad as late interpolations.

Perhaps these examples may suffice to indicate the manner in which constant accretions to and modifications of the Troy legend appear from age to age. It would be especially interesting to trace throughout the Hellenic period the figure of Achilles. He seems to have been regarded, possibly even from early times, as a type of the youthful beauty and chivalric courage which the race ascribed to itself. The more mystical belief, indeed, of a later time could not accept the Homeric story, that he had ever passed to the sunless land of ghosts. Instead, the fable arose that at Thetis' prayer the "White Island" was created for his abode in the far eastern seas; and there he yet tarries, fittingly mated with

Helen, and still gathering about him the gallant friends who had been his comrades before Troy. This fancy, though it contradicts Homer himself, I for one refuse to relinquish. The only Achilles who ever existed for me is living to-day in the fair Orient island of Homeric poetry.

The most remarkable instance, however, of a transplanted myth is the Roman belief in Æneas as the founder of their race. This belief it seems worth our while to trace out in somewhat fuller detail. There is no clear intimation in the Iliad that Æneas ever left Asia. Homer says (Iliad, XXII. 306–307) : —

Now shall the mighty Æneas be ruler *over
the Trojans,*
He, and his children's children, who shall
be hereafter begotten.

It may well have been pure accident that he did not say "at Troy" or "in the Troad." Whoever wrote these lines evidently knew of a royal race, ruling presumably in the Troad, which claimed descent from Æneas.   There is no hint of an emigration.

Arctinos, one of the " Cyclic " poets who in the ninth and eighth centuries B.C. pieced out Homer's story, says (Kinkel, Fragmenta Epicorum Græcorum, p. 49) that Æneas and his associates, horrified by Laocoon's death, fled to Ida the day before Troy fell.   According to Lesches, who wrote a rival supplement, called the Little Iliad, Æneas shared with Andromache the lot of slavery under Neoptolemos.   We shall see still a third legend traced to the early lyric poet Stesichoros ; namely, that Æneas escaped by sea and emigrated to " Hesperia."   Virgil attempts a sort of concordance of all these ancient statements ; but they show that the post-Homeric folk had no knowledge or tradition at all on the subject.

Sophocles, in his lost drama, Laocoon, is the first, so far as we know, to give the famous picture of Æneas carrying his father : —

Now at the portal of the goddess stands
Æneas with his father on his shoulders, —

S

> Over whose smitten back a linen cloak
> Doth flow, — and round about the house-
>   hold throng.
> Nor yet so great a multitude is gathered
> Of Phrygians, who this emigration crave.

Whither Sophocles sent them we do not know.

The statement that two towns in Sicily, Eryx and Segesta, were founded by Trojan wanderers, appears as early as Thucydides, who died about 400 B.C. (Thuc. VI. 2. See also Cicero against Verres, IV. 33, 72, with Long's note, Cic. Orat. Vol. I. p. 481).

The earliest attempts to connect Rome with any illustrious heroes of Oriental myth were apparently made by Greeks, eager to flatter the coming race, or to soften the shame of subjugation by barbarians. There is a perfect labyrinth of interwoven or contradictory legends on the subjects. Dionysios traced out most of them. The Evander-myth is gracefully used by Virgil. One story joined *two* famous wanderers, Odysseus and Æneas, in the enterprise. Heracles also was early made to extend his wanderings to Latium. These attempts are not in themselves unnatural. Real early colonies, like Cumæ, may have suggested mythical predecessors. There was even an actual kinship, of course, between Italic and Hellenic races, of which a faint consciousness may have lingered still.

But it will always seem strange that the representative of the sinful and vanquished race was finally accepted as the true ancestor, rather than *e.g.*, Ulysses, whose son by Circe, Telegonus, is mentioned in Horace as founder of the neighbouring Tibur. However, Æneas' high character in the Iliad, his escape and mysterious survival, made him a tempting subject. The westward spread of Aphrodite's worship carried with it her son's fame. Possibly the influence of Cumæ was also helpful, for the elder Kyme, in Asia, was Troy's neighbour, and a sort of heir to her traditions. There may have been also a direct influence from the Sicilian cities, especially in the first Punic war.

The Romulus-myth was accepted somewhat earlier among the Romans. It contradicted the Æneas-legend, and so was undoubtedly quite independent of it. It was itself needful as a link with Alba. That ancient head of the Latin League, though long ago destroyed, was kept in memory through the recurring sacrifices by the Latins on the Alban Mount. Hence the tale of

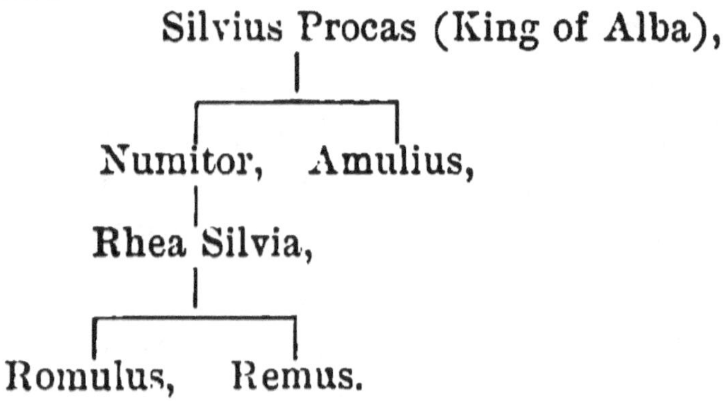

The bronze wolf nursing the twins was set up in 296 B.C. (It is perhaps a later copy that is now in the Capitoline Museum.)

But not long afterward Eastern conquest caused the Romans to see a use for such an ancestry through Æneas. The junction with the Romulus-myth is at first very awkward. Since both could not found Rome, Æneas is made father of Romulus, —or of Romulus' mother. (So both Nævius and Ennius.) Dionysios seems to credit

these stories to the annals of the pontifices
as their earliest source. The boys were en-
trusted, it was said, to the childless king
Latinus, and won his love and at last his
heritage.

But by Cato's time (ob. 148 B.C.) Romans had noted the great gap between
Troy's fall (1184 B.C. according to the
Greeks) and Rome's foundation (753 B.C.
by their own reckoning). So the Alban
kings must fill this gap with their shadowy
line, dimmer, and certainly less real, than
Banquo's descendant's. Some of them
may have existed before in the local Alban
tradition, — possibly even in the flesh.

This modification of the Æneas-myth
had at times an influence on Roman political action, and of course formed the corner-stone for the greatest of Latin epics.
It is especially interesting, therefore, to
note that the earliest authority we can
discern for any emigration of Æneas westward is Stesichoros, a Sicilian poet about
600 B.C.; and for our knowledge of this
important fact we are indebted to no direct
literary tradition at all, but to a work of

art. Furthermore, the relief in question
is not archaic, nor even of a good classical
period, but a late Roman work, probably
nothing better than a mnemonic school-
tablet recalling the chief scenes of the Trojan war. The central group of pictures
upon this tablet (the well-known Tabula
Iliaca) represents the destruction of Troy.
Æneas appears in three successive scenes,
the last time just embarking upon his ship.
The inscription for this latter group reads:
" Æneas with his folk setting off for Hesperia," while the chief central inscription
is: " The destruction of Ilios according to
Stesichoros."

Thus a tasteless Roman relief, which
perhaps stood in just such a smoky, com-
fortless schoolroom as Juvenal describes,
has, by some happy chance, drifted down
to us; and from this alone is supplied the
first link for the connection between the
greatest of Greek legends and the leading
myth of the Italian world,—a closing illustration of a thesis which needed no demon-
stration: " All are needed by each one."

APPENDIX

SYLLABUS FOR A COURSE OF SIX LECTURES ON THE LITERARY STUDY OF HOMER

INTRODUCTORY NOTE

THE chief preparation for any special study upon the Homeric poems, should be, naturally, a careful reading of the poems themselves. The present course of lectures will partly presuppose — partly undertake to accompany and encourage — such a reading. The lecturer will devote his time rather to sympathetic interpretation than to analytical criticism.

The translation of the Iliad into somewhat archaic English prose, by three English scholars, Lang, Leaf, and Myers, is to be recommended. The similar translation of the Odyssey, by Professor Butcher and

Mr. Lang, is still more widely known. We prefer, however, the simpler version in "rhythmical prose" by Professor G. H. Palmer.

The famous versions of Chapman and Pope are English classics, and as such are deserving of all attention and study. They are not at all trustworthy interpreters of the words, or the ideas, of Homer. Of the many more recent and comparatively faithful poetical versions, Bryant's, in blank verse, is the most accessible, and is not seriously misleading, the original being rather diluted than distorted. Bryant's worst mistake was in substituting the names of Roman gods for the Greek names. Lord Derby's version, also, is of interest. The renderings of the entire Odyssey and half the Iliad in Spenserian stanzas, by the late Mr. Worsley, are marvels of ingenuity and grace. The version of the Iliad was creditably completed by Professor Conington. Though of course in no sense literal, these renderings are nearer to the originals than would seem possible under such difficult conditions. Copious and judicious selections from most of these, and from several other Homeric translators, will be found in the attractive volume recently published by Professor Appleton of Swarthmore, Greek Poets in English Verse. Mr. Way's versions of Iliad and Odyssey in hexameters are little known in this country, but are most warmly praised by Prof. Moulton.

Under sympathetic criticism, perhaps the famous essays of Matthew Arnold, On Translating Homer, still deserve the leading place. The lecturer remembers, however, that he was himself originally most indebted, for stimulus toward the literary study of the poems, to the late Mr. J. A. Symonds' essays in his Greek Poets. But for all serious students the masterly little volume of Professor Jebb, Introduction to the Study of Homer, is indispensable. It is doubtless unequalled in any language, and though intended especially for classical students, is for the most part quite intelligible to all.

Mr. Lang's co-translator, Professor Walter Leaf, has published a Companion to the Iliad, intended to be used with their joint version. This gives nearly all the material available for a careful detailed study of the poem in English. Mr. Leaf is, however, a rather advanced radical on the "Homeric Question." That is, he believes, not only that the present Iliad is the work of various hands, but that the successive strata can still be accurately distinguished and pointed out. Mr. Lang is, on the contrary, the most conservative among competent living students of Homer. His stout volume Homer and the Epic often takes the form of a rejoinder to Mr. Leaf. A certain diffuseness was doubtless inevitably inherent in the subject, — perhaps in Mr. Lang's nature as well. Though the most scholarly of his many books, it has a goodly share of his wit and grace. Mr. Lang defends the essential unity of authorship in the Iliad, — though not without some concessions. The opening chapters of the two friendly foemen state the case at issue very clearly. The present lecturer is in reluctant agreement with Mr. Leaf and Professor Jebb in their general theory.

Any student who desires to follow farther the lines of thought suggested by the fifth lecture, will find the most faithful versions of foreign authors to be the most useful. Plato's Republic is delightfully rendered in the Golden Treasury series, by Davies and Vaughan. Conington's prose version of the Æneid is now accessible apart from his other works. The translations of Dante, by Professor Norton in prose, and by Longfellow in verse, are familiar to all. Upon the question of Hades and its location much curious and recondite material, and a plausible solution of the problem, are contained in the book of President William F. Warren, of Boston University, called Paradise Found.

The subject of the last lecture is better adapted for enjoyment than for analytical study. The artistic charm of Nausicaa is, however, excellently brought out in an unpretentious essay by Charles Dudley Warner, entitled Simplicity. (*Atlantic Monthly*, March, 1889.)

Some older students may wish to revive an earlier acquaintance with the Greek

text. They will find the small Clarendon
Press editions convenient and well anno-
tated (Iliad, by Monro; Odyssey, by Merry).
The larger and rather expensive edition of
the Iliad by Professor Leaf is one of the
best productions of English scholarship.

But little reference will be made to the
archæological questions raised by Dr. Schliemann's striking discoveries at Troy, Mykenæ, and Tiryns. The recent book by
Schuchhardt, translated by Miss Eugénie
Sellars, will be found more convenient and
compact than Dr. Schliemann's own costly
volumes. The excavations on the site of
Troy are still incomplete, and the discoveries have raised more problems than
they have solved. The final report upon
these investigations, by Dr. Dörpfeld, is
eagerly awaited.

Grote is still unrivalled as a historian of
Greece, and his chapters upon Homer, in
particular, are even now of prominence
and weight in every discussion of the subject. But his history needs, in nearly every
part, re-editing, in the light of the great
advance, since his day, in our knowledge

of classical antiquity. To understand better the general nature of Greek life and literary art, Jebb's Primer of Greek Literature, or his Classical Greek Poetry, should be read with care by the beginner. The larger Manual in most general use is doubtless Jevons' History of Greek Literature. This contains too much polemic discussion, too little sympathetic interpretation; but it is carefully and ably written. All such handbooks are safer after an acquaintance with the master-works themselves.

Upon nearly every field of classical studies, a helpful cross-light is constantly thrown by the monuments of ancient art. Even a student ignorant of German will find the thousands of illustrations in Baumeister's Denkmäler most instructive. In numberless cases they show clearly the conceptions formed by the historical Greeks of their heroic ancestors. Of the scanty direct illustrations dating from the Homeric age itself, Schuchhardt's volume contains nearly everything of importance.

It is hardly necessary to add that a whole

library of books and essays exists, treating from all possible sides the numberless problems suggested by the Iliad and Odyssey. Detailed investigations are still going on, especially in Germany. They are largely philological in character, and any real understanding of them requires familiar knowledge of both Greek and German. For the æsthetic appreciation of the poems, as poetry, the latest results of German scholarship are less indispensable.

LECTURE I

THE ILIAD AS A WORK OF ART

The Greeks possessed pre-eminently the artistic power, and a sense of harmony and enjoyment in life. Homer was the Bible, and the primer, of later Greece. The Marvellous is the most prominent element in the Iliad. Hardly any historical facts can be culled from the poem. The local geography is right; but the story seems purely ideal. Homer's individuality is quite lost: but he was certainly a conscious artist, probably a courtly minstrel.

This detachment from history perfects the poem artistically. The Iliad satisfies the three chief canons: unity, truthfulness, beauty.

Many features of the myth now familiar were unknown to the Iliad. An outline of the plot shows opportunities for an expansion of the poem by successive hands. Grote saw in it an original epic Achilleid, enlarged to an Iliad. Scholars are coming nearer to essential agreement along that general line. An analogy may be drawn from the kindred art of architecture, where unity of design does not prove unity of authorship.

SUGGESTIONS FOR PAPERS

1. Does the poem on the whole fulfil the announcement of the opening lines?

2. Is the interest of the reader diverted, exhausted, or stimulated, by the retardation of the crisis?

3. Do you discern, in a connected reading, excrescences which mar the outline of the plot?

4. Is the general spirit of the poem elevating in spite of the bloody battle scenes ?

5. Do you feel the workings of essential justice despite the quarrelling of the gods ?

6. Do you catch any glimpses of the poet behind his work ?

LECTURE II

WOMANHOOD IN THE ILIAD

The chief passages for this subject are to be found in Books III., VI., XXII. (and XXIV.). Homer's women are not portraits, but ideal types. The Greeks are homeless, and of the women-captives in their camp we catch but a few vivid glimpses. Within the city we meet repeatedly Hecabè, Helen, Andromache. The great series of domestic scenes in VI. seems hardly in its proper place. Hector should not return repeatedly, alive, after this parting.

Our regard for Hecabè is weakened by her acceptance of polygamy, and any sympathy felt for Helen is quite overshadowed by her sin. Andromache typifies most effectively the pathos of woman's lot in war. As a wife, she may appeal more powerfully to us than to the Greeks. The idealization of motherhood is not Hecabè, but Thetis. All these figures are, however, duly subsidiary to the epic plot.

SUGGESTIONS FOR PAPERS

1. Is Aphrodite, to Homer, a real person, or only passionate love personified ?

2. Does the poet forget Troy's sin in his sympathy for Hector and Andromache ?

3. Does the poet deliberately undermine our sympathy for Hecabè ?

4. Is the prominence and freedom of Homer's women greater than is credible for so violent an age ?

5. How far was Helen responsible at the beginning ?

6. Is Helen truly repentant at any time ?

7. Do you believe the same poet who wrote, *e.g.*, Iliad III., could have represented Helen happy, honoured, and womanly, at home in Sparta, years later, as she appears in the Odyssey ?

T

LECTURE III

ACHILLES AND PRIAM.—THE CLOSE OF THE ILIAD

The last book of the Iliad is almost a complete drama in itself. The opening lines are like an explanatory prologue. Then all the divine agencies are set in motion to bring Priam and Achilles together. Thetis, Iris, Hermes, are all busy as messengers. Hermes in person escorts the old king.

The culmination of agony and humiliation is reached, when the suppliant Priam kisses the hand which slew Hector and his other sons. The approaching doom of both Achilles and Priam throws a blacker shadow over the scene.

It would have been inartistic to break off abruptly when the strain upon the feelings is most intense. The return to Troy and the rites over Hector are, in some degree, an anti-climax, but a necessary one. The last line sums up the poem. The sole bulwark of the guilty city lies buried. The wrath of men has worked out the just decrees of fate.

SUGGESTIONS FOR PAPERS

1. Is there inconsistency, or only development, between the wrathful Achilles, and Achilles in bereavement?

2. Do books like VI. and XXIV. show with certainty their origin in a later and gentler age than the rest of the poem?

3. Is there a fatal flaw in the comparison to a cathedral, as used to illustrate the possibility of manifold authorship in an epic like the Iliad?

4. Does Homer show partiality for and against his own characters, *e.g.*, Thersites, Diomedes, Æneas, Hecabè?

5. Does the artist appear to you to analyze or grasp firmly the ethical meaning of his own scenes?

LECTURE IV

THE PLOT OF THE ODYSSEY

The Odyssey is a later work than the Iliad, from which it frequently borrows. The poem naturally falls apart into three sections : Books I.–IV., Telemachos in

Ithaca, and abroad searching for his father; V.-XII., Odysseus' adventures until he reaches Ithaca; XIII.-XXIV., meeting of father and son, and the restoration of both to their own. The adventurous homeward voyage of Odysseus has gathered around itself many tales of old folk-lore not originally told of this particular hero; and it also echoes, to some extent, the reports of early Ionian mariners returning from distant seas. The first four and last twelve books are comparatively realistic. The house of Odysseus, for instance, can be studied with some profit archæologically, beside the actual "palace" ruins in Tiryns. — The last book is a feeble anti-climax where none was needed, and was rejected as spurious even by ancient critics. The contrast with the conditions at the close of the Iliad is instructive.

SUGGESTIONS FOR PAPERS

1. Do the first four books seem to be a weaker and later addition?

2. Is the council of gods in Book I. a mere replica of that in Book V. ?

3. Where can Telemachos have been during his father's last two voyages?

4. Remark on striking resemblances between any myth in the Odyssey and any folk-lore tales of other races known to you.

LECTURE V

THE WORLD OF THE DEAD, IN HOMER AND OTHER POETS

This is a study of the Odyssey, XI., supplemented by the beginning of XXIV., and slight references elsewhere in Iliad and Odyssey. A difficult problem is the location of Hades. It is under our feet, yet Odysseus sails there in a ship. Did Homer know the earth was spherical? Virgil (Æneid, VI.) makes Æneas enter a cavern of southern Italy, and descend. Dante begins in a wood, the situation of which is not told, and *then* descends to Hell. His Purgatory, however, could be reached by sea.

Homer loves earthly life with all the fervour of happy youth, and is only able

to imagine a pale, unsatisfactory reflection
of it elsewhere. Virgil is more affected by
Oriental feeling, and describes the Underworld often with rapture. To Dante the
eternal life is infinitely more vivid and real
than earthly existence. Plato (Republic,
Books II.–III.) reproves Homer sternly for
teaching men to dread death.

SUGGESTIONS FOR PAPERS

1. Is Plato justified in saying the reading
of Homer would tend to make men cowardly ?

2. Do the dead in Homer enjoy *any*
advantages over living men ?

3. Is their condition made more pitiful
by their ignorance regarding matters in the
upper world ?

4. How do you reconcile Virgil's two
doctrines taught in Æneid, VI.; transmigra-
tion of souls, and eternal punishment ?

5. Do we still, to any extent, regard the
great poets as especially inspired, and gifted
with larger visions of life and death, than
other men ? *e.g.*, Does Shakespeare's Hamlet, or Tennyson's Crossing the Bar, affect
our beliefs, or only our imaginations ?

LECTURE VI

NAUSICAA. A STUDY OF HOMERIC GIRLHOOD

Odysseus' brief stay in Scheria is the culmination of his adventures in the world of enchantment. The Phæacians are superhuman, like the Giants and Cyclops. They are near to, and in familiar intercourse with, the Olympian gods. Their barks, needing no oar or sail, follow their will, " faster than the thought of man." On such a vessel they bring the hero home at last, in an all-night voyage, while he lies in dreamless sleep (Odyssey, XIII.). His refusal to tarry even here in Phæacia, as husband of a lovely princess, makes clear the prevailing motive of the whole poem : love of home.

The meeting of Odysseus, forsaken, shipwrecked, in utter exhaustion, with the happy, imperious, and beautiful maiden, is the boldest use of contrast in all Homer. The poet treats her with exquisite delicacy, drawing her with a simplicity which is the highest skill. She enjoys in his song the eternal youth of art.

SUGGESTIONS FOR PAPERS

1. Are there any touches of caricature in the account of the Phæacians ?

2. Is Nausicaa absolutely natural and childlike, or has she a tinge of coquetry ?

3. Does this episode bear either the marks of purely poetic invention, or any traces of a historical foundation ?

4. Is the passage at the beginning of Book XIII., deliberately intended to be taken as a transition from fairyland to reality ?

BIBLIOGRAPHY

This list contains all the books discussed in the Introductory Notes. The price given is the publisher's, or "list" price. With the exception of the Macmillans' publications, books are usually to be had at a discount of from fifteen to twenty-five per cent from these prices. The most useful works for the student are starred (*) ; those indispensable for careful study are doubly starred (**).

GREEK TEXTS, WITH NOTES

Iliad, edited by Monro, 2 vols. Macmillan	$3 00
Iliad, edited by Leaf, 2 vols. Macmillan	8 00
Odyssey, edited by Merry, 2 vols. Macmillan	2 20
Odyssey, Books I.–XII., edited by Merry and Riddell. Macmillan	4 00

TRANSLATIONS

Iliad, by Chapman. Morley's Universal Library	40

Iliad, by Pope.   Rutledge $1 25
Iliad, by Worsley and Conington .   21s.
Iliad, by Derby.   Murray $1 50
Iliad, by Bryant.   Houghton, Mifflin
   & Co. 2 50
** Iliad, by Lang, Leaf, and Myers.
   Macmillan 1 50
Iliad, by Way.   Sampson Low . .   18s.
Odyssey, by Worsley . . . . .   12s.
* Odyssey, by Butcher and Lang.
   Macmillan $1 50
** Odyssey, by Palmer.   Houghton,
   Mifflin & Co. . . . $1 50 and   1 00
Odyssey, by Bryant, 1 vol.   Hough-
   ton, Mifflin & Co. 2 50
Odyssey, by Way.   Sampson Low   7s. 6d.
* Greek Poets in English Verse,
   by W. II. Appleton.   Houghton,
   Mifflin & Co. $1 50

ELUCIDATION OF HOMER, ETC.

* Matthew Arnold's Essays in Criti-
   cism.   Holt & Co. 3 00
* Greek Poets.   J. A. Symonds.
   Smith and Elder 3 50
** Introduction to the Study of

Homer. R. C. Jebb. Ginn &
Co. $1 12

* Companion to the Iliad. W. Leaf.
Macmillan 1 60

* Homer and the Epic. Andrew
Lang. Longmans 2 50

GENERAL WORKS OF REFERENCE

Grote's History of Greece, Vols. I.–
XII. Murray 17 50

Holm's History, Vols. I. and II. Macmillan 5 00

Abbot's History, Vols. I.–III. Longmans . . . . 31s. 6d.

Curtius' History, Vols. I.–III. Bent-
ley . . . . £4 10s.

Oman's History of Greece . . . $1 50

Primer of Greek Literature. Jebb.
Am. Book Co. 35

History of Greek Literature. Jevons.
(Reprint by) Scribners 2 50

Baumeister's Denkmäler des Clas-
sischen Alterthums. I.–III.(about) 20 00

MISCELLANEOUS

Warren's Paradise Found. Houghton, Mifflin & Co.. . . . . . 2 00

Longfellow's Dante, 3 vols. Hough-
ton, Mifflin & Co.. . . . . . . $4 50
   One volume edition. Houghton,
   Mifflin & Co.. . . . . . . 2 50
* Norton's Dante, 3 vols. Hough-
ton, Mifflin & Co. 3 75
* Conington's *Prose* Translation of
Virgil. Longmans 2 00
Davies and Vaughan's Republic of
Plato. ("Golden Treasury.")
Macmillan 1 00
* Schliemann's Excavations, by C.
Schuchhardt. Translated by Eu-
génie Sellers. Macmillan . . . 4 00
New Chapters of Greek History, by
Percy Gardner. Putnam . . . 5 00

———

Note.—The author has permitted himself some freedom of revision in reprinting
this syllabus. In the present volume, parts
of the fifth lecture, referring to Virgil and
Dante, are omitted. (See the *Atlantic
Monthly* for July, 1884.)

Envoi

Homeros, or whatever name be thine,
Supreme magician of primeval song,
    Unrivalled master of the glorious line
That rises, rolls, and breaks, as free and
        strong
    As the great billows on a lonely beach; —
    If earthly voices yet may hope to reach
The far abodes of immortality,
    Forgive him, who in harsh barbarian
        speech
    Would echo — can but mock — thy won-
        drous melody.

The Iliad of Homer.

Done into English Prose by ANDREW LANG, M.A., Late Fellow of Merton College, Oxford; WALTER LEAF, Litt.D., Late Fellow of Trinity College, Cambridge, and ERNEST MYERS, M.A., Late Fellow of Wadham College, Oxford. Seventh Edition, revised.

12mo. Cloth. $1.50.

The Odyssey of Homer.

Done into English Prose by S. H. BUTCHER, M.A., Fellow and Prælector of University College, Oxford, Late Fellow of Trinity College, Cambridge, and ANDREW LANG, M.A., Late Fellow of Merton College, Oxford. Third Edition, revised and corrected, with Additional Notes.

12mo. Cloth. $1.50.

A Companion to the Iliad.

For English Readers. By WALTER LEAF, Litt.D., Formerly Fellow of Trinity College, Cambridge.

12mo. Cloth. $1.60.

Landmarks of Homeric Study.

Together with an Essay on the Points of Contact between the Assyrian Tablets and the Homeric Text. By the Rt. Hon. W. E. GLADSTONE, M.P.

12mo. Cloth. 75 cents.

MACMILLAN & CO.,

66 FIFTH AVENUE, NEW YORK.